JESS THE BORDER COLLIE
The Homecoming

Fraser Miles put an arm round Jenny's shoulders. 'We have to tell Mr Palmer everything we know, lass,' he said. 'How else can he make a diagnosis and help Jess?'

'Your father's right,' the vet agreed, his face sympathetic. 'The more I know, the better the chance of curing Jess.'

Jenny nodded miserably. 'It's just that Jess is usually so good. He would never bite anyone.'

'He's ill,' Tom Palmer said. 'Some illnesses can change a dog's character.'

Jenny swallowed her tears. She knew what it would mean if Jess was branded an aggressive dog – and she couldn't bear to think of it . . .

CONEMUR
ST. MARY'S
CHURCH OF ENGLAND
PRIMARY SCHOOL

JESS
THE BORDER COLLIE

THE HOMECOMING

LUCY DANIELS

ILLUSTRATED BY SHEILA RATCLIFFE

Hodder
Children's
Books

a division of Hodder Headline plc

Special thanks to Helen Magee

Text copyright © 1999 Ben M. Baglio
Created by Ben M. Baglio, London W12 7QY
Illustrations copyright © 1999 Sheila Ratcliffe

First published in Great Britain in 1999
by Hodder Children's Books

A Catalogue record for this book is available from the British Library

ISBN 0 340 73597 X

Typeset by Avon Dataset Ltd, Bidford-on-Avon, Warks

Printed and bound in Great Britain by
The Guernsey Press Co. Ltd, Channel Islands

Hodder Children's Books
a division of Hodder Headline plc
338 Euston Road
London NW1 3BH

1

Jenny Miles opened her eyes. For the first time in ages she was waking up in her old bedroom. Her spirits soared. 'I'm back at Windy Hill!' she shouted, as she leaped out of bed and went over to the window.

Down in the farmyard, pale February sunshine sparkled on the fresh green paint of the new lambing barn and bounced off the cobbles. Jake and Nell, her father's sheepdogs, trotted across the yard towards the barn, their plumy tails wagging as they followed Fraser Miles. Jenny hugged herself in happiness. It was as if she had never been away.

Her father turned and looked up at her window. He smiled, lifting his hand to wave, his dark hair ruffled by the wind. Jenny waved back, then turned to look around her. She could still hardly believe she was back in her own room. She had pinned a few posters to the newly-painted yellow walls. Her favourite photograph of her mother stood in a frame on a chair next to her new bed, while a new desk filled the space below the window where the old one had been. But the room still looked bare compared to how it had been before last November's terrible fire. The farmhouse had almost been destroyed.

Jenny sighed. Perhaps her room would never be exactly as it had been before, but that didn't matter. 'All that matters is that I'm back at Windy Hill,' she whispered, touching her mother's photograph gently.

'Jenny! Breakfast is almost ready,' called a voice from downstairs.

'Thanks, Mrs Grace,' Jenny called back to the housekeeper, then grinned as she heard barking. 'Morning, Jess!' she added, heading out of the door.

She hung over the newly-painted banister and laughed as she saw Jess, her black-and-white Border collie, gazing up at her as he waited patiently at the foot of the stairs. He'd had a habit of tilting his head to one side ever since he was a puppy. Now, with his white muzzle and a black patch over each eye, he looked adorable.

'I'll be down soon, boy,' Jenny told him, as she rushed into the bathroom.

Jess was still waiting when Jenny hurtled downstairs ten minutes later. He launched himself at her as she jumped the last two steps and she gave him a cuddle. 'Isn't it good to be home?' she said into his soft fur. Jess wagged his tail and licked her ear.

'It certainly is,' Fraser Miles said, coming in through the kitchen door. 'Jake and Nell are glad to be back in their old quarters.'

Jenny smiled up at her father. 'I thought you'd be out with the sheep by now,' she said. Fraser Miles ran a thousand Scottish Blackface ewes on their Borders sheep farm and lambing was only two weeks away – an especially busy time in the sheep farmer's year.

'Marion Stewart is dropping by,' her father

explained, as Jenny went through into the big, sunny kitchen. The walls, newly plastered and whitewashed, looked stark and cold, but Jenny's mother's old blue plates were back on the enormous dresser that stood against the far wall, and that brightened the kitchen up a little. The dresser had cleaned up well from the soot of the fire.

'The insurance company needs just one more signature to confirm that all the restoration work has been completed.' Mr Miles continued.

'And then we can get back to normal,' Mrs Grace said, as she put three plates of bacon, egg and tomatoes on the table.

Jenny nodded eagerly as she sat down to her breakfast. Mrs Grace had come to look after the Mileses after Jenny's mother had been killed in a riding accident almost two years ago. No one would ever take Sheena Miles's place but Ellen Grace had settled in so well that she seemed to belong at Windy Hill now.

'And thank goodness for that, now we're running into the busiest time of year,' Fraser said. 'The first lambs are due at the beginning of March.'

'I can help out as soon as the Easter holidays start,' Jenny offered. 'And Matt will get time off from college again this year for the lambing, won't he?' Jenny's brother, Matt, was nineteen and was away at college studying agriculture. He came home as often as he could to help out on the farm.

Her father nodded. 'The college treats it as part of his course,' he assured Jenny. 'I'll certainly be glad of his help – and yours too if you're serious about lending a hand.'

Jenny grinned. 'Try and stop me,' she said.

Jess butted Jenny's knee. 'Are you looking for my leftovers?' she said, rubbing his ears. Jess lifted one paw and tilted his head to one side. Jenny laughed, giving him a bit of bacon. Jess wolfed it down and then, happy that he'd got his titbit, went and lay down in his basket by the Aga. Mrs Grace shook her head. 'Mind you don't spoil him,' she said with a smile.

'I won't,' Jenny replied. 'He knows he only gets a treat from my plate after I've finished.' She looked at her father. 'Maybe Jess could help again this year. Remember how he wore a harness and took bottles of milk round to the orphaned lambs out in the fields last year?'

'That certainly was a sight to see,' Fraser said, smiling. 'Have you still got the harness you made for him?'

Jenny shook her head. 'It was lost in the fire. But I could make another one.'

'We'll see,' her father said. 'Things should be a lot easier this year now that we've replaced the lambing barn. There'll be fewer ewes having their lambs out in the fields.'

'You won't lamb all the ewes in the barn though, will you, Fraser?' Mrs Grace asked.

Fraser Miles shook his head. 'No, Ellen. I'll still be lambing in the fields, but I'll use the barn for the weaker ewes and the first-time mothers – and of course I'll be able to keep the orphaned lambs in there in the warming pens.'

Jenny knew that orphaned lambs had to be kept warm and needed to be fed by hand. The warming pens were like boxes with slatted lids. They had heaters underneath so that the tiny creatures wouldn't get a chill. The weather in spring in the Scottish Border hill country could be treacherous and new-born lambs often died of cold.

There was a tap on the door just as they were finishing breakfast and a youngish woman with short dark hair popped her head into the kitchen. It was Miss Stewart, the representative who had dealt with the insurance claim when the farm

THE HOMECOMING

burned down. It had taken a while to get the claim through, and so, over the past few months, Marion Stewart had been a regular visitor at Windy Hill. Jess ran to her, tail wagging. She looked down at him and patted him on the head. 'Good dog,' she said, then briskly brushed a hair that Jess had shed from her skirt.

Jenny called Jess to her. 'Sorry about your skirt, Miss Stewart,' she apologised. 'Jess isn't used to anyone minding about their clothes around Windy Hill.'

Marion Stewart always wore very stylish clothes. Today she had on a bright pink suit and was carrying a smart black briefcase. 'I met the postman as I arrived,' she said, handing Fraser a sheaf of envelopes. 'There seems to be quite a lot of mail.'

'Oh, more cards!' Jenny exclaimed. 'We've had so many to wish us a happy return to Windy Hill. There were six waiting for us when we arrived back.'

'Here's one for you, lass,' Fraser said. 'It's from Canada. And one for Ellen too.'

Mrs Grace poured Marion a cup of tea as Jenny tore open her letter. 'It's from Ian!' she cried, delighted. Ian Amery, Mrs Grace's nephew, had lived at Windy Hill for a time while his parents looked for a house in Canada. Now he had gone to join them. Jenny missed him but she had lots of other friends at school – especially Carrie Turner, her best friend.

Jenny glanced through her letter then looked up as Mrs Grace exclaimed. 'Oh! My sister, Maggie, has invited me out to Canada for a visit at the end of the month . . . In fact, she'd like me to stay until the end of March!'

Jenny felt a swift surge of disappointment that Mrs Grace might go away so soon after they had arrived back at Windy Hill.

'Then you should go, Ellen,' Fraser Miles said. 'It's a long time since you saw your sister, isn't it? And there's no point going all that way for only a few days.'

Jenny smiled and nodded. Her dad was right. 'Yes, Mrs Grace,' she said. 'You deserve a holiday.'

'But March is lambing time – the busiest time of year,' Mrs Grace protested. 'I'd hate to leave you in the lurch.'

There was a short silence, then Marion Stewart spoke up. 'I have a suggestion to make,' she began. 'I have a lot of holiday leave due to me. I could easily

9

take it when Ellen is away and help out at Windy Hill.' She looked at Fraser and smiled. 'I'm sure I could rustle up the odd meal or two. I did a cookery course at evening class in Greybridge last year.'

Fraser Miles raised his eyebrows in surprise. 'That's a very kind offer, Marion,' he said. 'But we wouldn't want to put you to any trouble.'

'It would be a pleasure, Fraser,' Marion assured him. She turned to Mrs Grace. 'So you can go to Canada as soon as you like, Ellen. And perhaps I could move into your room, while you're away, then I'd be on the spot. What do you think, Fraser?'

'That would certainly seem to make sense,' Fraser Miles responded. 'Is that OK with you, Ellen?'

Mrs Grace nodded, looking a little dazed at how quickly everything had been decided.

'Good!' Marion said, looking pleased. 'That's settled, then.' She looked at her watch. 'Now, Fraser, if you could just read and sign this form for me,' she said, taking some papers out of her briefcase, 'I'll have to be on my way.'

'You can open the rest of the cards, Jenny,' Fraser Miles said, handing them to her as Marion put the papers in front of him.

Jenny took the cards. 'This one is from Tom

Palmer, the vet,' she exclaimed, passing it over to Mrs Grace. 'And this one's from Carrie's mum and dad.'

Jenny picked up another card. It was addressed to her. 'It's from Fiona McLay,' she said as she read the message. 'It says, "Happy return to Windy Hill, from your grateful friend, Fiona." '

'That's kind of Fiona,' Mrs Grace said, starting to clear away. 'How is she getting on at school?' Fiona was in the same class as Jenny and Carrie. 'It must have been difficult for her going back after what happened.'

Jenny nodded. 'She's getting on fine now. But then, she's a lot nicer than she used to be.' Fiona McLay lived at Dunraven, the neighbouring farm to Windy Hill. She had bullied Jenny when they were younger and it had been Fiona's fault that Windy Hill had burned down. But the guilt had made Fiona very ill and she had been away from school for a long time. The only thing that had helped Fiona recover had been having Jess as a companion. And, for that, Fiona had been grateful to Jenny. During her recovery, Jenny and Carrie had visited Fiona often and had come to like the changed girl she had become.

Jenny's mind went back to Fiona's first day back at school a couple of weeks ago. The Mileses were still living at Thistle Cottage on McLay land at the time. Jenny had opened the front door on Monday morning to find Fiona and her mother, Anna McLay, standing there.

They had offered Jenny a lift to school. Fiona hadn't felt confident enough to take the bus straight away, and had confided how nervous she was feeling. Jenny had been happy to offer her support. Now she wondered at the change in Fiona McLay. It was amazing to think that this girl, who used to be the class bully, was now seeking help from her! She smiled as she remembered the fuss Fiona had made of Jess, when she'd seen him that morning. She seemed to really love the Border collie and had set off for school a lot more happily after seeing him. Within a few days Fiona had settled back into the school routine – though she did tend to cling to Jenny and Carrie a little now. But Jenny didn't really mind. It was a nice change.

'You're daydreaming, lass.' Her father's voice broke into Jenny's thoughts. 'You'd better hurry or you'll miss the school bus.'

Jenny picked up the last card. 'This one's for you,

Dad,' she said. 'It's marked "Personal".'

'What on earth . . . ?' Fraser exclaimed, as he opened the envelope.

Mrs Grace and Jenny glanced at each other in surprise. 'What is it, Dad?' Jenny asked, as she pulled on her coat.

Fraser Miles coughed, 'Oh, it's just a lot of nonsense,' he said.

Jenny looked over at the card and saw that there was a big red heart on it. She grinned. 'Dad, you've gone all red.' Her eyes lit up. 'Of course! It's February the fourteenth – Valentine's Day. Oh, Dad, have you got a valentine?'

Fraser Miles mumbled and pushed the card over to Jenny. 'I suppose I won't get any peace until you've seen it,' he said.

Jenny opened the card. Mrs Grace leaned over to have a look too. There was no signature, just a big 'M' in one corner.

'It could just be Matt having a joke,' Mrs Grace suggested. But Jenny noticed that she glanced across the table at Miss Stewart, who was busily packing the signed papers back into her briefcase. Jenny caught her breath. Carrie had always said that Miss Stewart had taken a fancy to her father.

Marion Stewart looked up at Fraser and smiled. 'Isn't that romantic?' she said.

Jenny watched her father and Marion as they smiled at each other. Suddenly Miss Stewart didn't seem to be in any great hurry to leave after all!

2

'Well, I reckon it *was* Miss Stewart,' Carrie announced, when Jenny told her and Fiona about the card at school that morning. 'I always thought she was after your dad.'

'Does it bother you, Jenny?' Fiona asked.

'It does a bit,' Jenny admitted. 'It's so weird – my dad getting a valentine card.'

'I can't imagine *my* dad getting an anonymous valentine card,' Fiona said. Jenny couldn't imagine that either. Calum McLay, Fiona's father, was so surly and unfriendly she couldn't imagine anyone ever sending him a valentine.

'I bet my dad would *love* to get a mysterious valentine card,' Carrie announced. 'And it would drive Mum mad. I wish I'd thought of sending one to him.' Jenny and Fiona laughed.

Then Fiona grew serious. 'Is it because of your mum that you don't like the idea of your dad getting a valentine card, Jenny?'

Jenny looked at Fiona, surprised at her understanding. Jenny still missed her mother very much. She nodded and, feeling a little upset, looked away.

Fiona flushed. 'I'm sorry,' she said. 'I've got no right to interfere.'

'No, it isn't that, Fiona,' Jenny replied quickly. 'You're right – thanks. And thanks for your welcome home card, too. It was really nice of you.'

Fiona flushed even more. 'You're welcome,' she murmured.

'I guess we're a threesome now,' Carrie said, sliding an arm through Jenny's and the other through Fiona's. 'Look, Dad has asked if we'd like to go out to Puffin Island on Saturday. Is everyone keen?' Carrie's dad ran boat trips to Puffin Island, a nature reserve just off the coast.

Jenny shook her head. 'I'd love to, but Matt is coming home this weekend and I promised I'd help with the sheep, now it's so close to lambing time. His girlfriend, Vicky, is coming to help too.'

'Oh, well,' said Carrie. 'We'll just have to be a twosome this weekend!' she joked to Fiona.

'I'm really looking forward to it,' Fiona said excitedly. 'I've never been before.' Jenny and Carrie had been surprised to discover that Fiona was interested in wildlife.

'Well, I'm sure you'll have a great time,' Jenny said. Though it did feel odd that Carrie would be spending the weekend with Fiona and not her.

When Jenny arrived home from school that afternoon, there was another surprise waiting for her.

'I've booked my ticket to Canada,' Mrs Grace said. 'The only flight I could get was next Monday.'

'But that's so soon,' Jenny protested.

Mrs Grace nodded. 'I've got so much to do before then,' she said worriedly. 'I have to pack up Ian's things and do some shopping for myself. It's just as well Marion Stewart is coming to help out. She's even offered to cook dinner for all of us on Saturday, so I can get on with other things.'

'That's nice of her,' Jenny agreed, then added, laughing, 'It sounds as if we'll be in good hands while you're away!'

Mrs Grace smiled back. 'I can't disagree with that!' she replied.

Marion Stewart arrived just after lunch on Saturday. She was wearing jeans and a very expensive looking sweater instead of her usual smart suit. Mrs Grace had gone into Greybridge for a couple of hours to do some last-minute shopping and to pick up her tickets for Canada.

'I'll take Jess for a walk this afternoon if you're helping with the sheep, Jenny,' Miss Stewart offered.

'Thanks,' Jenny replied. 'I'm sure Jess would love that.'

'You don't know what a help this is, Marion,' Fraser Miles said, shaking his head. 'How can I thank you for it?'

'You could take me out to dinner one evening,' Miss Stewart replied, smiling up at him.

Fraser Miles smiled back. 'That would be a

pleasure,' he said. 'Just name the day.'

Now Jenny was *sure* that Miss Stewart had sent that card! But before she could dwell on this development any further, she heard the sound of Matt's motorbike turning into the yard and everything else was forgotten. She whirled round, dashing out of the front door, Jess barking excitedly at her heels.

Her brother was helping his girlfriend Vicky off the bike. 'Matt!' she cried.

'Hi, Jen!' Matt responded, picking her up and swinging her round. He put her down again, his blue eyes laughing at her. Jess leaped up at him, wanting his share of Matt's attention, and he bent towards the Border collie to ruffle his coat. Jess licked his face.

Jenny turned to the slim, fair-haired girl who was unfastening the luggage from panniers on the side of the bike. 'Hi, Vicky!' she said. Vicky was doing the same course as Matt at agricultural college.

'Hello, Jen. It's nice to see you again – and Jess!' Vicky replied as Jess jumped up at her. She looked up at the farmhouse. 'I can't wait to see inside!'

'Let's go in then,' said Matt.

'Wait a minute, Matt,' Jenny said. She had to ask,

just to be sure. 'Did you send Dad a valentine card?'

'No way!' Matt laughed. 'I only sent one valentine card.' He grinned, looking at his girlfriend.

'It was very romantic,' Vicky said, blushing.

'So does that mean Dad's got a secret admirer?' Matt asked, surprised.

Jenny nodded. 'Mrs Grace and I think Marion Stewart sent it. The card was signed with a big M.'

Matt gave a low whistle. 'The next few weeks should be interesting, then,' he said, an amused glint in his eye.

Mrs Grace arrived home from Greybridge late that afternoon, loaded with carrier bags. Fraser Miles was pulling into the farmyard with Jenny, Matt and Vicky in the back of the jeep. Jess shot out into the yard.

'Hello, boy!' Jenny cried as the Border collie threw himself at her, almost knocking her over. 'Have you been waiting for us? Did you have a good walk?' She hugged him. The young sheepdog wagged his tail so hard he overbalanced and sat down heavily beside her. Jenny laughed. 'That reminds me of when you were a puppy,' she said. Jess had been the smallest puppy in the litter – the runt, her father had called him. He had been born with a twisted leg and had to have it in a plaster cast for weeks to straighten it. He had always been falling over then. But the treatment had worked and now no one would guess there had ever been anything wrong with him.

'Come on, boy!' Jenny urged, taking one of Mrs Grace's bags. 'Let's get this stuff inside.' Jenny offered a small plastic bag to Jess and he took it gently in his mouth, then trotted across to the kitchen door.

Mrs Grace laughed. 'Good boy, Jess!' she called. Jess wagged his tail proudly and disappeared into the house.

'We'll be right behind you,' Fraser called, as he and Matt strode across the yard with Jake and Nell. 'I want Matt and Vicky to give me a hand shifting some sacks of concentrate.' Jenny nodded. The ewes were very near to lambing now and needed extra feeding.

As Jenny followed Mrs Grace into the kitchen, a delicious smell met her. Marion Stewart stood at the oven. Her normally tidy hair was a little ruffled.

'That smells wonderful,' said Mrs Grace.

'How has Jess been, Miss Stewart?' Jenny asked, as Jess trotted across the kitchen floor and gave her the plastic bag he'd been carrying.

'I took him up to Darktarn,' Marion Stewart replied. 'We had a great time, didn't we, boy?' She held out her hand to pat Jess but the Border collie scampered out of reach.

Jenny looked at Jess in surprise.

'What's wrong with Jess?' Mrs Grace asked.

Jenny bent down and ruffled Jess's ears. 'I don't know,' she said. 'He's usually so friendly.'

'Maybe he doesn't trust me yet,' Miss Stewart said brightly. 'But he'll get used to me.'

Jenny frowned. Jess was usually such a friendly dog. She turned to Miss Stewart, a little embarrassed at Jess's behaviour. 'Thanks again for taking Jess out,' she said. 'He loves going up to Darktarn. That's one of my favourite places too. And I'm sure you're right – he'll soon get used to you.'

Miss Stewart nodded. 'Now,' she said. 'Sit down, Ellen. Everything is done.'

Ellen Grace sat down at the table. 'This is very kind of you, Marion.'

Marion Stewart smiled. 'I might as well start as I mean to go on,' she declared.

At that moment the door opened and Fraser came in with Matt and Vicky.

'How was the shopping?' Vicky asked.

'Exhausting,' Mrs Grace replied.

Fraser Miles walked across the kitchen and lifted the lid of a saucepan. 'That smells delicious,' he said.

Marion smiled. 'It's carrot and ginger soup,' she said. 'And breast of chicken in a herb crust to follow.'

'Wow!' said Matt. 'We don't usually have such fancy cooking.'

Marion smiled again. 'Oh well, I hope you enjoy it,' she said.

Mrs Grace laughed. 'I'm sure we all will,' she said.

'It will be quite a treat! I'm rather a plain cook,' the housekeeper explained.

'But a good one, Ellen. I love your cooking!' Matt said, putting his arm round Mrs Grace.

'Flatterer!' Mrs Grace replied. But she seemed pleased. 'I'll just put these things away,' she said, picking up some carrier bags.

'I'll help,' Jenny offered. 'Come on, Jess.' The Border collie scampered after them.

'Mrs Grace,' Jenny said, as they unpacked the bags of shopping, 'I'm going to miss you while you're away.'

Ellen Grace smiled. 'I know that, Jenny,' she said. 'And I'll miss you too – but you'll have Marion here.'

'Yes, I know,' Jenny replied. 'And she seems really nice. But I'm *used* to you. I can come home and tell you everything that happens at school – and I know Jess is happy here with you – and I don't even know if I *like* carrot and ginger soup,' she finished, breathlessly.

Mrs Grace laughed. 'Give it a try,' she said. 'You might love it.'

Mrs Grace was right. Jenny did love Marion

Stewart's cooking. 'That was delicious,' she said as she put down her soup spoon.

Marion put the main course in front of them. Jenny looked at the small piece of chicken in the centre of her plate. There was a small heap of garden peas and a few tiny potatoes beside it. It looked lovely, but there was so little of it! She looked over at Matt.

He sat there, open-mouthed, then said, 'Is this all there is?'

'Er, it looks delicious, Marion,' Mrs Grace said. 'But I usually make quite a hearty meal – a roast dinner or a shepherd's pie – in the evening. A day out in the fields works up the appetite,' she explained apologetically.

'Now, don't be so ungrateful, Matt,' Fraser chided. 'We can always fill up with bread and jam afterwards, if we're still hungry.'

Matt nodded and cheered up a little. Vicky smiled. 'I know it sometimes seems as if Matt's got hollow legs,' she said ruefully, as a rather deflated Marion turned away to fetch the water jug. 'But even *I* feel ravenous after a day in the fields.'

'What there is really does taste great, Marion,' Matt complimented her, as he tucked in.

'I hope you like it too, Fraser,' Marion said.

Fraser looked down at his plate. He had nearly finished. 'I must do,' he said. 'It's almost all gone!' he joked.

Jenny giggled. Her father usually ate at least twice as much when he came in from the fields.

'Perhaps we could go out on our dinner date tomorrow, Fraser,' Marion suggested.

'But it's Mrs Grace's last evening before she goes to Canada,' Jenny protested.

'That's true,' Fraser Miles put in. 'But I'm sure you and Ellen would like a cosy evening together before she flies off to Canada. What do you say, Ellen?'

'I can't think of anything nicer,' Mrs Grace replied, smiling.

'Thanks, Ellen,' Fraser said, looking pleased. 'That's a date then, Marion.'

Marion smiled up at Fraser and flicked a tiny speck of fluff off his sleeve. 'I'll look forward to it,' she said.

3

Matt and Vicky had gone back to college the following evening, when Fraser Miles came downstairs dressed for his dinner date with Marion. He looked very smart.

'You look really nice, Dad!' Jenny exclaimed, as Jess ran to meet her father.

'I hardly recognised you, Fraser,' Mrs Grace joked. 'It's quite a change from your usual farming clothes. Now, be careful Jess doesn't get dog hairs all over your trousers. Marion wouldn't like that.'

Jenny called Jess to her and gave him a cuddle. She had forgotten how handsome her father could look when he was all dressed up. Then Jenny noticed that her father was carrying a box under one arm. She recognised it. It was her mother's jewellery box.

'I found this when I was rearranging my things upstairs,' Fraser said. 'I think it's time you had it, lass.'

Jenny felt tears prick her eyes as she took the box from her father and opened it. She looked inside at the familiar earrings, bangles and necklaces. In her mind's eye, Jenny saw her mother wearing them. She missed her so much. 'Thanks, Dad,' she whispered.

Jenny turned to Mrs Grace. 'Sometimes Mum used to let me try her jewellery on,' she said. 'She laughed when I decked myself out in all her bangles and necklaces.' Jenny took out her favourite necklace, a delicate gold chain interlined with aquamarines. She clasped it round her neck.

There was a sound at the door and Marion Stewart looked into the room. 'I hope I'm not early, Fraser,' she said brightly.

'Not at all, Marion,' Fraser replied. 'Come in.'

As Marion came into the room Jess immediately moved away. Jenny couldn't understand it. Jess was still uneasy around Miss Stewart.

'My goodness, Jenny, that's a lovely necklace!' Marion Stewart exclaimed.

'It certainly is,' Mrs Grace agreed. 'It was Jenny's mother's. Sheena had some lovely things.'

Jenny put her hand to the necklace and looked up at Marion. 'Mum's grandmother left it to her. Great-Grandma left Mum all her jewellery.'

Marion Stewart smiled. 'Your father has told me a little about your mother. She sounds like a wonderful person.'

'Oh, she was,' Jenny said, taking off the necklace and putting it safely back in the box.

'Ready, Fraser?' Marion asked, reaching up and straightening his tie.

Fraser Miles nodded and gave Jenny a quick pat on the shoulder as he escorted Marion to the door.

'Enjoy yourselves,' Mrs Grace called after them as they left, then she turned to Jenny and smiled. 'Your father seems to like Marion a lot,' she said thoughtfully.

★ ★ ★

When Jenny ran downstairs on Monday morning, Jess launched himself at her in his usual boisterous fashion. She found her father and Mrs Grace in the kitchen. 'How was your date, Dad?' she asked.

Fraser Miles flushed slightly. 'I wouldn't call it a date, lass,' he said.

'Marion called it a date,' Mrs Grace teased.

Jenny looked curiously at her father. He seemed embarrassed.

'We had a very nice meal,' Fraser admitted. Then he looked at his watch. 'Marion should be here again, soon.'

As he spoke, the door opened and Marion came in, two large suitcases in her hands. 'Good morning, everyone,' she said, smiling.

'Here, let me help you with those,' Fraser said, and he took the suitcases upstairs.

'I've cleared out my room ready for you, Marion,' Mrs Grace said. 'I hope you'll be comfortable.'

'I'm sure I shall be, Ellen,' Marion replied. She reached out to pat Jess. But, as before, Jess shied away.

'Jess!' Jenny exclaimed, embarrassed at Jess's behaviour. 'Say hello to Miss Stewart.'

'Don't worry about him, Jenny,' Marion said

brightly. 'He'll have plenty of time to get to know me while you're at school. After I've settled into Ellen's room, I'll take him for a walk.'

Jenny nodded. 'Thanks, Miss Stewart. I hope you had a good time last night.'

Miss Stewart smiled. 'Wonderful,' she said, smiling at Fraser as he came back into the kitchen.

Ellen Grace went to the window. 'That's Anna now,' she said. Anna McLay had offered to take the housekeeper to the airport.

A moment later Mrs McLay came in. 'We'll have to go, Ellen,' she said. 'We don't want you to miss your plane.'

Fraser Miles picked up Mrs Grace's suitcases and went with them out into the yard. Jenny and Miss Stewart followed.

'Oh, Ellen,' Mrs McLay said, as they loaded the boot. 'I've been meaning to ask you. Did you ever come across my diamond and ruby ring while you were working at Dunraven?' For the time that Windy Hill was being repaired, Mrs Grace had divided her time between the McLays' house, Dunraven, and Thistle Cottage, where the Mileses had stayed.

Ellen Grace frowned, then shook her head. 'I

remember the ring,' she said. 'You wore it at Christmas and I remember remarking how nice it was. But I would have told you if I'd found it lying around. Have you lost it?'

Anna McLay nodded. 'It's worth quite a lot of money,' she said. 'But it has even more sentimental value. I've looked for it everywhere.'

'I'm sorry I can't help, Anna,' Mrs Grace said. 'It really is a lovely ring. I hope it turns up.'

Anna McLay smiled and closed the car boot. 'Don't worry about it. Now we'd really better go.'

'Have a good trip, Ellen,' Fraser said, giving her a hug.

Mrs Grace smiled, then turned to hug Jenny. 'Goodbye, lass,' she said. Jenny hugged her back, hard.

Then Mrs Grace turned to Marion Stewart. 'Thanks again, for helping out, Marion,' she said. 'With you here to look after things, I don't suppose they'll even notice I've gone!' she joked.

But Jenny was quite sure she would miss Mrs Grace – and so would Jess.

'So they went out on a date!' Carrie exclaimed on the school bus half an hour later. Jenny had just told Carrie and Fiona about her weekend.

Jenny nodded. 'I think Dad really likes Miss Stewart,' she confided.

'Well, we had a great time at Puffin Island,' Fiona said. 'Didn't we, Carrie?'

Carrie nodded enthusiastically. 'And we're going to the cinema next Saturday afternoon. You will come, won't you, Jen?'

Jenny shook her head. 'The first lambs are due soon,' she explained. 'I want to give Dad a hand.'

'Oh, Jenny!' Carrie said frustratedly. 'We'll hardly ever see you out of school if you're going to spend every weekend helping with the sheep!' She turned to Fiona. 'Shall we go and have a burger after the cinema? There's a new place just opened in Greybridge.'

Jenny listened to them discussing their plans and sighed. Carrie seemed quite happy with just Fiona's company nowadays. They didn't seem to need her at all.

But a couple of weekends later, Jenny got a surprise. Early on the Saturday morning, Vicky turned up with Matt.

'So if you want a day off, I can take your place,' Vicky said to Jenny.

'That's a good idea,' Miss Stewart put in. 'You could take Jess for a walk, Jenny. I want to get some serious cleaning done today.'

'He looks as if he needs a walk,' Vicky agreed, going over to Jess. Jess licked her hand and wagged his tail.

Jenny looked at the Border collie lying in his basket. She'd noticed he spent a lot of time in his basket when Miss Stewart was around. He still hadn't accepted her. 'I'll phone Carrie, then,' she said. 'We can take Jess to Cliffbay. He loves a run along the beach.'

But when Jenny rang Carrie, her mother, Pam Turner, told her that Carrie wasn't there. 'She stayed overnight at Dunraven,' Mrs Turner explained. 'You'll get her there.' Jenny put down the phone, disappointed.

'What's wrong?' asked Miss Stewart.

'Carrie's staying with Fiona,' Jenny replied. She frowned. 'She didn't mention she was doing that this weekend.'

'She probably forgot,' Miss Stewart said reassuringly. 'Why don't you ring her at Dunraven?'

Jenny hesitated. 'I don't want to butt in if I'm not wanted.'

'Oh, Jenny, surely Carrie wouldn't think you were butting in,' Miss Stewart replied. 'She probably thinks you're too busy to see her.'

But still Jenny didn't want to phone Dunraven. After all, Fiona hadn't invited her.

'Why don't you take Jess for a walk up to Darktarn and then you can go and help out in the fields this afternoon,' Miss Stewart suggested. 'I'll be here so Jess won't be lonely.'

Jenny jumped up. 'Good idea!' she said. 'Come on, boy!'

★　★　★

Going to Darktarn *was* a good idea. The old Border keep had been a favourite place with Jenny and her mother and going there always made Jenny feel better. As Jess ran ahead, Jenny stood and let the wind blow through her hair. From up here she could see the whole of Windy Hill laid out below her and, far in the distance, the sea sparkled in the sunshine.

By the time Jenny returned to the farm she was feeling a lot better.

'You've changed your mind, have you?' Fraser Miles asked, when he, Matt and Vicky popped home for lunch.

'We'll be glad of your help,' Matt added. 'We're going to check the first-time mothers to see if any of them are likely to give birth early and we'll pen the ones that look like lambing first in the lambing barn.'

When it was time to leave, Jenny looked around for Jess. He was in his basket again. She walked over and gave his ears a rub. She was almost certain that Jess was spending so much time in his basket because he didn't like Marion. But why?

'What's on the menu tonight, Marion?' Matt asked, as he and Fraser made for the door.

Marion gave him a brilliant smile. 'It's a surprise, Matt,' she said.

Matt nodded. 'Oh, well, it's sure to be good – and the more the better, by the way,' he added cheekily.

'Come on, Matt,' said Vicky, pushing him out of the door. 'See you later, Miss Stewart.'

The young ewes were nervous and skittish. Jake and Nell had to work hard, rounding them up without scaring them.

'Away to me, Nell,' Fraser said to his dog, as Matt sent Jake far out across the field in the opposite direction. Jenny watched, fascinated, as the two dogs raced across the short grass, their plumy tails streaming out behind them.

'Jake will get behind them,' Fraser Miles explained. 'He'll make sure none of them bolt. Then Nell will round them up so that we can get them into the holding pens.'

Jenny nodded. Jake was the outrunner, able to hear and obey commands from a long distance while Nell was best close in to the sheep, driving them on towards the pens.

'Get the gate, Jenny,' Matt said, as the flock began to move. Jenny hauled open the gate of the holding pen while Nell picked off the ewes Fraser had selected and shepherded the sheep into a column, guiding them through the gate. Matt and Vicky got behind them, driving them towards the pen.

As the last ewe of the group entered the pen, Jenny closed the gate and watched while her father and Matt examined the ewes, judging which ones were likely to give birth first. Then those were separated off into another pen and the process began again. By the time they had finished they had more than fifty ewes to drive down the track to the lambing barn and Jenny was kept busy with the gates and rounding up the odd straggler. It was getting dark by the time they got the last of the young ewes safely housed in the lambing barn and made their way towards the house.

Jenny called to Jess and the Border collie came running towards her.

Marion was taking a roasting pan out of the oven and Matt looked at it in amazement. 'Roast beef!' he said. 'And roast potatoes.'

'And Yorkshire puddings,' Marion added proudly. 'I thought you would approve!'

'How right you are, Marion,' Fraser said, coming into the kitchen. 'I don't suppose Matt's hints had anything to do with it, did they?'

'Sit down and rest, Fraser,' Marion laughed, as

Matt turned red. 'You look tired.'

'Not a bit of it,' Fraser insisted, going towards her. 'Let me help you, Marion.'

As Miss Stewart bustled about, putting the food on the table, Jenny looked at her father, helping Marion carry plates and serving spoons to the table. Her father and Marion seemed friendlier than ever.

'Is anything wrong, Jen?' Vicky asked softly.

Jenny shook her head. 'Not really,' she said slowly. Then she turned to the other girl. 'Vicky,' she said, lowering her voice, 'do you think Dad and Miss Stewart are in love?'

Vicky looked a little surprised. She frowned. 'I think Miss Stewart is definitely interested in your father,' she said at last. 'But love – I don't know, Jenny.'

Jenny sighed. She didn't know either.

4

When they'd finished eating, Jenny offered to do the washing up. Matt and Vicky had gone out to the stable to see Mercury, Matt's horse. Jess was scampering around the kitchen.

'He's very lively tonight,' Fraser Miles remarked, as Jess ran past Marion, who was clearing the table, and over to Jenny, leaping up at her.

'*Down*, Jess,' Jenny said, as she took the washing-up liquid from its shelf. Her hand brushed against a clear plastic packet and it fell on to the counter, spilling some of its powdery contents. 'Oops!' she said, looking at the packet. 'What's this? Is this yours, Miss Stewart?'

Marion went quickly over to the counter and picked up the packet, putting it back on the shelf. 'Yes,' she replied, sweeping the spilt powder into her hand and into the sink. 'It's from the herbalist – for my headaches.'

'I didn't know you got headaches,' Fraser Miles said, surprised.

'I don't like to complain,' Marion replied. Then, suddenly, Jess ran up to her, barking sharply and snapping at her hand.

'Jess!' Jenny cried, shocked.

Marion snatched her hand out of the way.

Fraser Miles leaped up. 'Jess! Basket!' he bellowed. Jess immediately ran to his basket and lay down. Then Fraser turned to Marion. 'Are you OK?' he asked.

Marion nodded. 'He didn't hurt me.'

'He shouldn't have snapped,' Fraser Miles said seriously.

Jenny looked at Marion. Suddenly she remembered another time when Jess had acted so strangely. It was with Fiona McLay after the fire last November. Jess had been in the house when Fiona had set it on fire and had tried to tell them who was to blame. But it was ridiculous to think that Jess knew anything bad about Marion!

'I don't see why he should have taken against you like this,' Fraser Miles went on to Marion. 'You've been looking after him and feeding him for the last two weeks.' He held out his hand to her. 'Let's go and relax in the living-room.'

As her father and Marion passed Jess's basket to go to the living-room, Jenny saw Jess draw back. Something was definitely bothering him.

Jenny dried her hands and went across to him, kneeling down. She stretched out her hand and stroked his head. 'What is it, boy?' she asked. As she looked carefully at him, Jenny drew in her breath. Jess was trembling. Jenny laid her hand on his side. She could feel tremors running right through him. Suddenly Jess's chest heaved, and he yawned widely. Then he began to shake violently and uncontrollably.

'Dad!' Jenny yelled. 'Dad! Come quickly. There's something wrong with Jess!'

Jenny rushed to the door but her father had heard

her shouts and was already there as she opened it. He went swiftly over to the Border collie, as Matt and Vicky arrived.

'We heard the shouting. What is it?' Matt asked, alarmed.

Fraser Miles turned, his face serious. 'Jess is having a fit,' he said. 'Ring the vet, Matt. Tell him it's an emergency.' Wrapping Jess's blue blanket around him, he picked the Border collie up and carried him over to the Aga, calling, 'Jenny, get another blanket. And Vicky, bring Jess's basket.'

Jenny rushed to the dresser and heaved open the bottom drawer. She pulled out a blanket and raced over to Jess. Behind her, she could hear Matt's urgent voice speaking to Tom Palmer, the vet.

Vicky scooped up the basket and placed it on the rug in front of the Aga. Fraser Miles laid Jess down in it gently. 'We must keep him warm. Shivering like that can mean his body temperature is dropping.' Jenny wrapped the extra blanket tightly round Jess.

Fraser turned to Jenny. 'Has this happened before?' he asked.

Jenny shook her head, too upset to speak.

Fraser turned to Marion Stewart who was

standing by the kitchen table. 'Has anything like this happened while you've been looking after him, Marion?' he asked.

Marion shook her head. 'But he has snapped at me before,' she admitted. 'I didn't want to say anything, but I do find his aggressiveness worrying.'

'Aggressive!' Jenny echoed, horrified. 'Jess has never been aggressive.'

'He must be ill,' Matt said firmly.

Fraser nodded. 'But you should have mentioned Jess's aggressiveness to me, before, Marion,' he said.

'I didn't like to,' Marion Stewart explained. 'After all, I'm not used to dogs. I thought it was my fault – that he just didn't like me – and besides, you've been so busy with the sheep, I didn't want to worry you.'

'That was very thoughtful of you, Marion,' Fraser said. 'But the sooner Tom Palmer sees Jess the sooner we'll know exactly what's wrong with him.'

Jenny bent over Jess again. The shaking was becoming less violent and gradually, as Jenny watched, it began to fade away, leaving Jess lying limply in his basket. His eyes began to focus again and he looked up at Jenny pitifully.

'Oh, Jess, what's wrong with you?' Jenny

whispered, putting her arms round him. Even through the blankets, she could feel occasional tremors running through him. She looked at her father. 'He won't die, will he?'

Fraser Miles put his arm round her shoulder. 'Of course not,' he said reassuringly.

'Maybe he's got a bug,' Matt put in. 'Let's just wait and see what Tom Palmer has to say.'

The next half-hour seemed the longest of Jenny's life as she sat by Jess and watched the tremors slowly fade away altogether. At last Jess's eyes drooped and he fell asleep. By the time Mr Palmer arrived, Jess seemed to be breathing more easily.

As Tom Palmer examined him, he shook his head. 'I don't quite know what has happened here,' he said. 'His breathing is a bit shallow and his heart rate is a little erratic but that's only to be expected after a fit.' He looked at Jenny. 'This hasn't happened before?'

Jenny shook her head.

'No, but he *did* seem a bit excitable tonight. And he's also been aggressive with Marion recently,' Fraser Miles said quietly.

'He's snapped at me a few times now,' Marion Stewart confessed. 'And he's seemed a bit nervous – jittery, I would call it. But then I'm not an expert.'

'You don't have to be,' Tom Palmer told her. 'You're being very helpful. If Jess has been aggressive, I need to know about it.'

Jenny looked at her father. 'You know Jess is the best-tempered dog in the world,' she protested.

Fraser Miles put an arm round Jenny's shoulders. 'We have to tell Mr Palmer everything we know, lass,' he said. 'How else can he make a diagnosis and help Jess?'

'Your father is right,' the vet agreed, his face sympathetic. 'The more I know, the better the chance of curing Jess.'

Jenny nodded miserably. 'It's just that Jess is usually so good. He would never bite anyone.'

'He's ill,' Tom Palmer said. 'Some illnesses can change a dog's character.'

Jenny swallowed her tears. She knew what it would mean if Jess was branded an aggressive dog – and she couldn't bear to think of it.

'Of course, he *was* the runt of the litter,' Fraser Miles said. 'There's often a flaw in the smallest pup. He didn't have an easy birth. I suppose there could have been other damage besides his leg.'

'You mean brain damage,' Tom Palmer said, looking serious. 'That certainly is a possibility. He could have been suffering from a weakness from the very beginning and something has triggered it – perhaps a virus. That's most likely.'

'So what can we do?' asked Matt.

Tom Palmer spread his hands. 'If it's a virus there isn't much to be done except wait for it to work its way through. I'll take a blood sample and run some tests to see if anything shows up. We'll also have to wait and see whether the fits recur. Perhaps the problem will sort itself. If it doesn't and there's a permanent tendency to aggression, then we'll have to think again. But we need to give it time before we consider doing anything drastic.'

'What do you mean by "drastic"?' Jenny asked, horrified. Tom Palmer looked at her, his eyes full of compassion. Jenny turned pleadingly to her father. When Jess had been a newly-born pup Fraser Miles had thought the best thing would be to destroy him. Was that what Mr Palmer was suggesting now? 'But, Dad, Jess has always been perfectly healthy apart from his leg.'

Fraser Miles didn't say anything for a moment. 'He's always *seemed* healthy,' he said at last. 'This illness could just have been waiting to happen.'

'Poor thing,' Marion Stewart sympathised. 'Does this mean he'll have to be put down? I know I'm not an expert on dogs but I wouldn't have thought you could afford to keep an aggressive dog on a sheep farm.'

Jenny drew in her breath sharply. Miss Stewart had voiced the thought that had been in all their minds. Jenny turned to Tom Palmer desperately. 'No!' she cried. 'You saved his leg, Mr Palmer. You operated on him when he was just a puppy. You can't put him down just because he's had a fit.'

'Now, now, Jenny,' Tom Palmer said. 'Don't get yourself so worked up. This might never happen again. Let's just wait and see.'

'But if it does happen again?' Jenny insisted.

Mr Palmer looked at her seriously. 'Well, lass, if the fits keep recurring, Jess wouldn't have much of a life. And he might become a danger – to people and other animals. He wouldn't be the Jess you know and love any longer.'

Jenny looked at the vet, horrified. 'You mean if Jess goes on having fits you might really have to put him to sleep?'

'For his own sake,' Tom Palmer said gently.

Marion Stewart leaned across and touched Jenny on the shoulder. 'It would be kindest to Jess,' she said.

The tears streamed down Jenny's cheeks. How could it ever be kind to kill Jess? 'I'll love Jess whatever he does,' she said through her tears.

5

Jenny woke early next morning and slipped quietly downstairs, pulling on a dressing-gown as she went. No one else was up yet and Jess was still fast asleep in his basket. Jenny settled herself down beside him, but she didn't touch him. She was afraid to disturb him.

It was an hour before anyone else appeared. Her father walked softly into the kitchen and found her still sitting silently beside Jess's basket.

Fraser looked down at Jess. 'He seems to be breathing normally,' he said.

Jenny nodded.

Her father gave her a hug. 'I remember finding you down here with Jess when he was just a tiny pup,' he said. 'You'd got up to feed him and you were both fast asleep.'

Jenny brushed a hand across her eyes. Jess had needed to be hand-fed for the first few weeks of his life but Jenny had never minded getting up in the middle of the night to feed him. 'He *will* be all right, won't he, Dad?' she asked, desperately.

'Tom is a good vet,' her father said. 'He'll look after Jess. Now you go and get dressed.'

Jenny rose reluctantly and went back upstairs. When she returned, Jess was still sleeping. Matt and Vicky were in the kitchen and Miss Stewart was preparing breakfast.

'Vicky and I are going out to the fields with Dad soon,' Matt told Jenny. 'Are you going to stay with Jess this morning?'

Jenny nodded. She couldn't bear to think of leaving him while he was so ill.

'Come and have some breakfast, Jenny,' Miss Stewart said.

But Jenny could hardly eat for worrying about Jess. She forced down a piece of bacon and tried to listen to her father talking about the lambing to Matt and Vicky.

Suddenly there was a sound from Jess's basket and Jenny shot out of her seat and bent down beside him, her heart thudding. Slowly, Jess opened his eyes. Catching sight of Jenny, he licked her hand then went to sleep again. Jenny breathed a sigh of relief. At least he had woken up briefly. She had begun to think he might sleep for ever.

'We'll have to be off,' Fraser Miles said. 'I think we'll have our first lambs soon.'

Matt and Vicky rose from the table and, as Vicky passed, she gave Jenny a sympathetic smile, bending down to stroke Jess. 'I hope he gets better soon,' she said softly.

Jenny nodded, tears pricking her eyes. 'So do I, Vicky,' she said fervently. She picked up Jess's food and water bowls to take them to the sink. 'Maybe he'll feel like something to eat and drink when he wakes up properly,' she said. 'I'll wash these out.'

There was a powdery mark on the floor where Jess's food bowl had been. Vicky grabbed a cloth and wiped it.

Jenny smiled her thanks as Vicky grabbed her coat and ran out to join Matt and Fraser in the jeep. Nell and Jake were in the back, their plumy tails wagging. The dogs loved their work. Jenny waved as her father drove out of the yard.

'If you want to go out with your father this afternoon, I'll look after Jess,' Miss Stewart offered.

Jenny shook her head. 'I'll stay here with Jess to-day,' she replied. 'I couldn't leave him the way he is.'

'You'll have to leave him to go to school tomorrow,' Miss Stewart warned.

'I know,' said Jenny. 'But maybe he'll be better by then. Maybe if he eats and drinks something, it'll help.'

During the afternoon Jess woke up properly and managed to drink a whole bowl of water and eat some finely minced meat that Jenny prepared for him. And by the time Fraser, Matt and Vicky came home at the end of the day, the Border collie seemed almost back to normal, though he was still a little tired.

'That's good news, Jen,' Matt said, as he and Vicky got ready to go back to college.

Jenny smiled up at him from her place by Jess's basket. 'Let's hope he'll be even better tomorrow.'

* * *

With a heavy heart, Jenny tore herself away from Jess to go to school next day. As soon as she got on the school bus, Carrie noticed something was wrong. 'What is it?' she asked. 'You look upset.'

Jenny sat down in the seat in front of Carrie and Fiona. 'Jess had some kind of fit on Saturday,' she explained.

Carrie and Fiona both looked shocked. 'Oh, poor Jess,' Carrie cried.

'Has the vet seen him?' Fiona asked.

'Of course,' Jenny replied, slightly irritated by the

question. Fiona sometimes seemed to act as if Jess was hers. 'He says the fit might just be a one-off,' Jenny continued. 'But . . . if not, if he starts to bite . . .' she couldn't go on.

'What?' asked Fiona, then her eyes darkened in horror. 'Oh, no, Jenny. You don't mean he would have to be put down?'

Jenny nodded wordlessly. Carrie laid a hand on her arm. 'It won't come to that, Jen,' she said.

'It can't. Not Jess,' Fiona added.

Jenny looked at Fiona. The girl's eyes swam with sudden tears. She had grown very attached to Jess during her illness – almost too attached. At one point Jenny had thought she might lose Jess to Fiona altogether.

'He could come to Dunraven,' Fiona offered. 'Mum would look after him while you're at school, Jenny.'

'No,' Jenny said quickly. 'Miss Stewart is there to look after him. And Jess is happier in his own home.'

'That's true,' Carrie agreed. 'Can we come and visit him, Jenny?'

Jenny nodded. 'Of course.' She swallowed hard. 'This morning was the first time he's ever stayed in his basket when I left for school. Usually I have to shut the gate on him to make sure he doesn't follow me.'

Carrie leaned towards her. 'Try not to worry,' she said. 'Maybe it was just something he ate.'

'I suppose it could have been that,' Jenny said. 'Oh, I hope that's all it is.' Carrie's words made her feel a little better.

'And, if it was, then he'll be better soon,' Carrie continued. 'You can bring him to our next sleepover. Fiona and I had good fun but it would have been even better with you and Jess.'

Jenny looked at Fiona and Carrie, sitting together as if they had always been friends, and couldn't help feeling a little left out. Then she flushed, remembering that she had avoided phoning Dunraven, thinking that they might not want her around. As it was she was glad she'd been at home when Jess had fallen ill. But Jenny couldn't help wondering whether Fiona would really have wanted her there over the weekend. Perhaps she enjoyed having Carrie to herself . . .

Jenny spent the day worrying about Jess, but when she got home he seemed back to his old self, running to her as soon as she got in the door.

'Carrie thought it might have been something he ate,' she said to Marion, as she hugged Jess. 'You aren't feeding him anything different, are you, Miss Stewart?'

'I hope I know how to feed a dog,' Miss Stewart said sharply.

'Sorry,' Jenny said quickly. 'I think Carrie was just trying to make me feel better,' She sat back on her heels and let Jess lick her face. 'Anyway, I don't care what it was so long as it's over,' she said, looking at Jess's bright eyes.

Even so, Jenny woke early next morning and ran downstairs to check on Jess. The Border collie leaped up from his basket and scampered over to her, wagging his tail. Jenny opened her arms to him, relieved that he still seemed well.

'Maybe Carrie was right,' she whispered in his ear. 'Maybe you ate something you shouldn't have. I hope so.'

By the time her father came down, Jenny and Jess were playing happily on the floor, Jenny tossing a ball for him. 'Up early again, lass?' he said.

'I was still worried about Jess,' Jenny explained. 'But he seems fine.'

'He certainly does,' Fraser agreed, smiling. 'And

I've got a surprise for you,' he said. 'I went out to check on the young ewes last night before I went to bed. We've got our first lambs – twins.'

'Oh, Dad, can I see them?' Jenny asked excitedly. 'And can Jess come too?'

Fraser bent and rubbed Jess's ears. 'Of course he can.'

Jenny dressed in double-quick time and followed her father out to the lambing barn, a lively Jess at her heels.

'There,' said Fraser, as he opened the door.

Jenny looked into the nearest pen. There were two tiny black-faced lambs snuggled into their mother's side, fast asleep.

'Oh, Dad, they're beautiful,' she said. 'Look, Jess.'

Jess poked his nose through the bars of the pen and snuffled as Jenny gazed at the new-born lambs.

'That's only the start,' Fraser Miles said. 'We've got a busy time ahead of us.'

Jenny smiled. She knew her father didn't mind the hard work. The lambs were worth it.

Carrie and Fiona came home with Jenny after school the next day. Jess raced out to meet them.

Jenny felt uncomfortable as she watched Fiona

fussing so much over Jess. She was glad Fiona loved Jess, but Jess was *her* dog, not Fiona's.

Anna McLay called in some time later to pick up the two girls. She was going to drive Carrie home on the way to Dunraven. 'It's good to see Jess looking so much better,' she smiled. 'Fiona was very worried about him. She couldn't love him more if he was her own dog.'

'What's wrong?' Carrie asked, seeing Jenny frown as she heard this.

Jenny shrugged. 'Nothing,' she replied. Her feelings were too complicated to explain, even to Carrie.

Just then, the phone rang. It was Mrs Grace. She was shocked to hear of Jess's illness and rang again the following evening to see how he was doing. Ian said he was sending a get well card to Jess even if he couldn't read it! And Matt rang home every day too.

Marion Stewart was surprised by all this attention. 'Jess certainly seems to be a popular dog,' she said to Jenny.

Jenny smiled. 'Everyone loves Jess,' she said.

Marion nodded thoughtfully. 'So it seems.'

The phone rang again and Jenny picked it up.

This time it was Tom Palmer. 'I got the results of the blood tests, Jenny,' he said. 'Nothing significant showed up, so it's my guess it was a virus. How is he?'

'He's back to his old self,' Jenny told him.

'That's very encouraging,' Mr Palmer said. 'Let's hope that's the last we'll see of it then.'

Jenny rang off and sighed with relief. Then she remembered that she hadn't asked the vet if it could have been something Jess ate. She put it out of her mind. Jess was well again. That was the important thing.

But when Jenny arrived home from school on Thursday there was no Jess running to meet her. Jenny's heart skipped a beat. 'Jess?' she called, as she dumped her schoolbag in the porch. There was no answering bark.

Jenny rushed into the kitchen. Marion was standing by the Aga looking serious. 'I'm afraid Jess has had another fit, Jenny,' she said.

Jenny ran to Jess's basket. The Border collie lay there, twitching slightly. He looked up at her and tried to raise his head but it seemed too much of an effort for him. He dropped his head heavily back down on his blanket.

'Oh, Jess,' Jenny said miserably. 'I thought you were better.'

'The fit didn't last long,' Marion said. 'But he *was* very agitated. He snapped at me.' Miss Stewart looked down at her hand.

Jenny drew in her breath as she saw the dressing that covered the woman's wrist. 'Did Jess do that?' she asked.

Marion nodded. 'But it hardly bled,' she assured Jenny. And, luckily, I've just had my anti-tetanus jabs renewed.'

Jenny turned back to Jess. 'Oh, Jess,' she said softly. 'What's happening to you?'

Marion Stewart came to stand over her. 'Perhaps we should call in Tom Palmer again,' she suggested.

Jenny looked up at Marion Stewart, tears standing in her eyes. She shook her head. 'I don't want to tell Mr Palmer about it – not yet. You said you weren't badly hurt. Can't we give Jess another chance – a chance to get well?'

Marion put her hand on Jenny's shoulder. 'I know what you're afraid of, Jenny,' she said. 'But you must think of what's best for Jess. If these fits go on, his life will be miserable. And you have to think of the consequences. What if he bit a child?'

Jenny bent over Jess again and stroked him. His eyes were closed now and he was sleeping, his breathing regular. 'Mr Palmer says he doesn't know what's causing the fits,' she continued desperately. 'But if this fit wasn't so bad, maybe he'll just grow out of them. Mr Palmer says the only thing to do is wait and let him rest. He'll get better. He's *got* to get better.'

Marion Stewart sighed. 'Let's hope so, Jenny,' she said. 'For his sake.'

'So you won't send for Mr Palmer?' she asked.

'Not this time,' Marion Stewart promised.

Jenny looked up at her. 'Oh, thank you, Miss Stewart,' she said. 'You'll never know how grateful I am to you for giving Jess another chance.'

'Why don't you call me Marion?' Miss Stewart said. 'We're friends, aren't we?'

Jenny nodded. 'Oh, yes,' she said. 'And just wait. Jess will get better soon and then you'll see what he's really like. He's the friendliest dog in the world and he'll just love you – once he's better.'

Marion didn't say anything for a moment. 'Don't get your hopes up too much,' she said at last. 'Sometimes it's best to be prepared for the worst.'

But Jenny wouldn't allow herself to do that – she couldn't imagine life without Jess.

When Fraser Miles arrived home he took Miss Stewart's injury very seriously. 'Let me have a look at it, Marion,' he said. 'Maybe you should see a doctor.'

Marion put her hand behind her back. 'Don't fuss, Fraser,' she said, smiling up at him. 'It was only a scratch.'

Fraser looked worried. 'We can't have Jess biting,' he said. 'And we certainly can't ask you to look after him now, Marion.'

'Nonsense,' Marion said briskly. 'I'll be more careful how I handle him now. Don't worry.'

Jenny looked at Marion gratefully, wondering why she was still so keen to look after Jess. She must really like him, Jenny thought.

Jenny could hardly concentrate at school next day.

'At least the Easter holidays start tomorrow,' Carrie comforted her. 'You'll be able to spend lots of time with Jess then.'

Jenny nodded. 'But I've promised to help Dad with the lambing, and I don't want to let him down.'

'I could look after Jess for you,' Fiona offered.

Jenny knew Fiona was trying to help but she shook her head. 'Thanks, but I couldn't bear to think of him anywhere but at Windy Hill,' she said. 'And if he is really ill, Dad won't expect me to leave him.'

Jenny ran all the way down the track from the bus stop after school and rushed into the kitchen, hardly able to ask the question that was hovering on her lips. 'Has he been all right?' she asked Marion, as she went at once to Jess's basket.

'He hasn't had another fit but he's been very sleepy,' Marion informed her.

'He didn't try to bite you, did he?' Jenny asked anxiously, as she bent over Jess and stroked him. Jess slowly opened his eyes and groggily lifted his head to lick Jenny's hand. Then, after a few seconds, he heaved himself up and clambered out of his basket, wagging his tail.

'He didn't have the energy to bite,' Marion said. 'That's the first time he's moved all day.'

Jenny gathered Jess into her arms. 'Gently, Jess,' she whispered. Jess licked her face again. He might be ill but he was still glad to see her.

And, the following morning, his tiredness of the previous day seemed to have gone. Jess scampered across the kitchen floor to Jenny. She bent down and threw her arms around him. 'Oh, Jess, you're so much better!' she cried, burying her face in his neck. 'And I won't have to leave you to go to school for a whole two weeks.'

'Jess certainly is a lot livelier this morning.' Fraser Miles said, coming in at the kitchen door with Marion. Jenny smiled up at them, overjoyed at Jess's improvement. 'And there's another surprise,' her father continued. 'Look who's here.'

Jenny leaped up as Matt walked through the door. 'Matt!' she cried.

'I got away earlier than I'd hoped, Jen,' Matt said. Then he bent to pat Jess who was standing patiently, tail wagging. 'How are you, boy?' he asked, as he rubbed Jess's ears. He looked up at Jenny. 'He looks well.'

'He's much more like his old self today,' Jenny told her brother. 'I'm beginning to see a pattern. He has a fit, then he's really tired the next day, and then it's as if nothing has happened – he's back to normal.'

'So are you coming to give us a hand with the lambing today?' Fraser asked.

Jenny hesitated. 'I'd like to,' she said. 'But I hate to leave Jess.'

'We'll take him with us,' her father announced. 'That'll give Marion a break from looking after him. He can stay in the jeep but you'll have to keep him on the lead if you want to walk him. I don't want him running loose in among the sheep.'

Jenny nodded. She knew her father couldn't take any risks where the pregnant ewes were concerned. 'I'll take him for a walk up to Darktarn at mid-morning break,' she said, delighted. 'You'd like that, wouldn't you, boy?'

Jess gave a short bark and wagged his tail. Jenny put her arms round his neck and gave him another cuddle.

'But I don't mind looking after Jess if you want to leave him here with me,' Marion said.

'I know,' Jenny replied. 'And I really appreciate that after Jess snapping at you the way he did. But maybe some fresh air will do him good.'

Marion looked a little disapproving. 'Well, I'm not sure about that,' she replied. 'Be careful you don't overtire him. That could bring on the fits again.'

'I won't,' Jenny assured her, as she followed her father and Matt out of the door.

'Marion is being really understanding about Jess,'

Fraser Miles remarked, as they made their way across the yard. 'You like her, don't you?'

Jenny nodded. 'Of course I do,' she replied.

Her father looked pleased, and again Jenny wondered what was happening between him and Marion. She turned to Jess and smiled as he ran to her, his eyes bright once more. 'Come on, Jess,' she called. 'We're going lambing!'

6

'Oh, isn't it gorgeous?' Jenny exclaimed, as the just-born lamb struggled to its feet.

Matt laughed softly. 'I never get used to this,' he said. 'It'll always be a miracle.'

Jenny watched as the ewe licked her little black-faced lamb all over, stimulating his blood supply, then the tiny creature nuzzled at his mother and fastened on her teat, beginning to suck.

Jenny turned to Matt. 'That birth went well,' she said.

Matt nodded, then he looked up. 'Dad is waving to us,' he said. 'Let's see what he wants.'

Jenny and Matt made their way across the field. Fraser Miles was bending over a ewe. The sheep was lying on the ground, her legs stiff, and her body heaving with effort. As Jenny watched, the animal began to strain even more, raising her head and curling back her top lip.

'This one is going to need some help,' Fraser Miles said.

Jenny looked at her father in concern. She knew that he would never interfere unless it was necessary. 'What's wrong, Dad?' she asked.

'This ewe is quite an elderly lady now,' Fraser said. 'This will be her last lambing and it's a bit of strain for her. I reckon we've got twins here.' He laid a hand on the ewe's flank. 'There, there, old girl, it won't be long now.'

Matt opened his lambing bag. 'What do you need, Dad?' he asked.

'The lambing oil,' his father answered, rolling up his sleeves.

Matt handed the bottle to his father and Fraser

rubbed the oil on his hands and forearms. 'Can you hold her head, Jenny?' he asked.

Jenny went to the ewe's head and took it in her arms. She had done this before. When a ewe had trouble giving birth she needed help to guide the lamb out of the birth canal, but it was a frightening experience for the animal.

Jenny talked gently to the frightened animal as her father and Matt worked.

'I thought so,' Fraser said. 'There are two lambs in here and I don't think she has any strength left to push them out. We'll have to pull them out for her, Matt.'

Jenny held her breath as her father gently eased out the first lamb and laid it on the grass. Matt immediately began to scrape away the membrane of the birth sac so that the lamb could breathe. A tiny black nose appeared, followed by two black front legs.

As he worked, Matt checked the lamb over. 'This one is all right,' he said.

Fraser Miles looked at Jenny. 'How's she doing, Jenny?'

Jenny looked down. The ewe's eyes were closed and her body was trembling. Suddenly she gave a jerk and was still. Jenny looked up. 'Oh, Dad,' she said, suddenly frightened.

Matt leaned over and put his hand on the ewe's side, his face serious. 'You'd better hurry, Dad,' he said, his voice strained. 'I'm afraid we've lost this one.'

Fraser Miles looked up, his eyes dark with sorrow. 'She was a good ewe,' he said softly. 'This is her fifth season. I never get used to losing a ewe.'

Jenny looked down at the sheep. The creature lay still, its head heavy in her arms. 'Poor thing,' she said with a break in her voice.

Matt looked at her sympathetically. 'It's hard, Jenny,' he said. 'But we've got to try and save the other lamb.'

Jenny nodded and blinked the tears away. Lambing could be very sad sometimes.

Fraser Miles set to work. Jenny looked across at him. His face was beaded with sweat as he eased and pulled at the lamb, trying not to damage the little creature still inside its mother's womb.

At last he gave a final pull and another little bundle slithered out on to the grass. At once Fraser began to tear the birth sac away, then reached into his lambing bag again, bringing out a rough towel to rub the tiny body in order to stimulate the blood supply. Jenny knew that usually the mother would do this by licking her lamb. She looked down sadly at the ewe for a moment, then took a deep breath. The ewe was beyond help but her lambs would need all the care and attention they could get if they were going to live.

'We've got to get these two into the lamb warmer as soon as possible, Matt,' Fraser said. 'They'll need to be hand-reared.'

'Matt can take me down in the jeep and I'll look after them,' Jenny said.

Fraser nodded. 'Be as quick as you can, Matt,' he said.

Matt and Jenny carried the new-born lambs to the jeep and wrapped them in a blanket to keep them warm, before tucking them safely in a box in the back. Jess sniffed them interestedly, then licked Jenny's hand. 'We're going back now, Jess,' Jenny said, as she got into the jeep.

Matt dropped Jenny off at the farm, turning straight back to the track. 'See you later,' he called as he drove off.

Jenny nodded as she carried the lambs in their box towards the lambing barn, Jess at her heels.

'There there,' she said as the tiny lambs bleated weakly. 'You'll soon be warm and fed.'

Jenny pushed open the door of the lambing barn, carefully shutting Jess outside. 'I know you wouldn't harm the lambs, Jess,' she said to him as he looked up at her. 'But I promised Dad I wouldn't let you in among the sheep.'

Jenny left Jess whining outside the door and moved down the barn. One end was taken up with pens housing young ewes that were about to give birth for the first time. Her father and Matt would come down later to check on their progress and make sure the ewes bonded to their lambs. That meant putting mothers and lambs in individual pens until the lambs were feeding regularly and the new mothers had got used to looking after them.

Jenny went over to the warming pen, and lifted the lid. She smiled as three furry black noses peeped out at her and the little Blackface lambs bleated piteously up at her. There would be a lot more orphaned and abandoned lambs in here before the lambing was done, but the warming pen was safe and cosy, and in a few days these lambs would be strong enough to come out into ordinary pens. She gently laid the new lambs in the pen and took an old rough towel from a hook on the wall. One at a time she rubbed the lambs down and breathed a sigh of relief as she saw them struggle to their feet, falling over almost at once but trying again.

'You're going to be all right,' she whispered to them. 'I'll be back in a minute with a bottle for each of you.'

With Jess at her heels, Jenny ran for the kitchen. 'I need to make up feeds for two new lambs,' she said as she rushed in.

Marion Stewart turned to her and smiled. 'Why don't you show me? Then, any time you're busy, I can help out.'

Jenny showed Marion the little bottles they used to feed new-born lambs, 'Dad keeps a supply of frozen colostrum to give to new-born orphaned lambs too,' she explained. 'That's the milk that the ewe produces immediately after she gives birth. The lambs need that for the first twenty-four hours so that they get all the antibodies they need to protect them against infection. We have to feed them every four hours at the beginning. Sometimes, if they're very weak or aren't sucking properly, it's every two or three hours.'

'That sounds like hard work!' Marion exclaimed,

looking rather less enthusiastic.

'It is,' Jenny agreed, 'but it's worth it. I would have been coming down soon anyway to feed the lambs that are already in the warming pen. I'll feed the newest ones first, then do the others. Can I leave Jess with you?' she asked.

'Of course you can,' Marion replied, moving towards Jess. The Border collie backed away, growling low in his throat.

'Jess!' Jenny exclaimed.

Marion shrugged, then backed away, looking at the bandage on her hand.

Jenny flushed. 'Maybe he's still got traces of that virus,' she said. She turned to Jess. 'Here, boy!' she said. 'Into your basket.'

Jess scrambled into his basket and looked up at her. 'Stay!' Jenny commanded.

Jess lay down, his head pillowed by his front paws, looking at Jenny pleadingly as she made up the feeds. Jenny tried to ignore him but it wasn't easy to avoid his big dark eyes and he whined when she made for the door.

'No, Jess,' Jenny said firmly as he tried to follow her. 'Stay!'

Jess crouched down in his basket again but his

ears were pricked and Jenny noticed that his hackles were slightly raised. She ran over to him and stroked his neck. 'There, boy,' she said softly. 'I'll be back soon.'

'He'll be all right,' Marion assured her. 'After all, he'll have to get used to me, won't he?'

Jenny smiled. Marion was so understanding. 'Thanks,' she said. 'I won't be long.'

Jenny hurried across to the barn and went immediately to the warming pen to offer the bottles to the new arrivals. They fastened on the bottles and began to suck. Jenny sat back on her heels, feeling the lambs pulling at the teats on the bottles.

She thought of their mother in the top field. It was sad when a ewe died but her two new lambs were healthy enough. She smiled. 'You'll be all right,' she whispered to them, as they finished their feed. 'I'll look after you.'

Jenny raced back to the kitchen and looked in at the door. Marion smiled at her. 'Your dad rang on the mobile,' she said. 'He and Matt are coming down to check the ewes in the lambing barn so he says you're to wait here for them.'

Jenny nodded and called to Jess. The Border collie ran to her and she hugged him. 'He's been good, hasn't he?' she asked Marion hopefully.

'I just left him alone,' Marion said. 'He seemed a little agitated after you left so I thought it was best.' Jenny rubbed her face against Jess's neck. She had a feeling that Marion had left Jess alone because she didn't trust him. 'You go and attend to the other lambs,' Marion went on. 'I'll feed Jess and, if he'll let me near him, I'll take him for a walk later.'

But Jenny saw her glance worriedly at Jess. Marion definitely didn't trust him.

Jenny spent the afternoon helping her father and Matt in the lambing barn. There were five new mothers and their lambs settled in pens by the time Fraser Miles called a halt.

'Let's see if Marion will give us a cup of tea,' he said.

'I could do with one,' Matt agreed.

'And I want to see how Jess is,' Jenny said, giving a new-born lamb a cuddle before she put it into the pen with its mother. The ewe immediately began to nuzzle the little creature, nudging it towards the farthest corner of the pen and settling down with the lamb sucking on her teat.

'That one seems happy enough,' Fraser remarked. 'I reckon we've earned our break.'

But when they pushed open the kitchen door, Jenny knew at once that something was wrong as soon as she looked at Marion Stewart's face. 'Is it Jess?' she asked.

Marion nodded. 'I was just coming to get you,' she said, turning to Fraser.

Jenny hurried over to Jess's basket and knelt down. 'It's just like before!' she cried.

Jess was lying shivering uncontrollably in his basket. Jenny ran to get another blanket from the dresser and wrapped it round him, trying to comfort him.

'What exactly happened, Marion?' Fraser asked.

Marion shook her head. 'I don't really know,' she said. 'I was busy upstairs and when I came down he was like this. I've only just found him.'

Jenny looked up, tears stinging her eyes. 'I don't understand it,' she said. 'He was all right earlier on.'

'This can't go on for ever, Jenny,' her father said seriously.

'I know that,' she said miserably. 'I know it can't go on.'

Next day was Sunday and Carrie phoned early. 'Can you take a day off from the lambing, tomorrow?' she asked. 'Dad's taking Fiona and me out to Puffin Island again. Do you want to come?'

'I can't, Carrie,' Jenny replied. 'We're so busy.'

'You sound worried,' Carrie said. 'Is Jess all right?'

'He's very sleepy this morning,' Jenny told her. 'He had another fit yesterday.'

'Oh, no! Was it the same as before?' Carrie asked, concerned.

'I wasn't there,' Jenny explained. 'Marion was looking after him.'

'Did you ask her if she was feeding him any differently?' Carrie asked.

'Yes,' Jenny replied. 'I asked her that, but she got quite annoyed with me. She seemed to think I was implying that she didn't know how to feed Jess properly.'

'So it's not something he ate,' Carrie concluded.

'No,' Jenny agreed. 'How could it be?'

But as Jenny said goodbye to Jess before going lambing with Matt and her father she wondered. Something had to be causing Jess's fits – but what was it?

By evening, Jess seemed to be getting a little better.

Fiona phoned, anxious about him. 'Carrie told me about the latest fit,' she said. 'How is he?'

'He's getting better again, now,' Jenny answered. 'There seems to be a pattern to it. He has a fit, then he's sleepy next day, then he's completely back to normal the day after. So I'm hoping he'll be fully recovered again tomorrow.'

And sure enough, the following morning, Jess was back to normal.

Fiona called again to ask after Jess. 'So he's all right now,' she said, sounding relieved. 'Are you going lambing today?'

'I expect so,' Jenny replied. 'Jess will be all right with Marion.'

'Would it be all right if I came to see him soon?' Fiona asked.

'Of course,' Jenny replied.

'If you change your mind you can always come to Puffin Island with us – Jess too,' Fiona offered, before she rang off.

Jenny had a good day helping her father and Matt out in the fields. But when they returned to the farmhouse late that afternoon, Jess didn't race out to meet them. Alarmed, Jenny jumped down from the jeep and ran into the kitchen. She looked at Jess's basket. It was empty. There was no sign of the Border collie anywhere. Her heart in her mouth, Jenny ran into the hall, up the stairs, calling Jess's name. There was no answering bark and Jenny ran back downstairs, stumbling in her rush.

'What's happened?' Matt asked, catching her as she hurtled out into the farmyard.

'It's Jess,' Jenny told him, her face white. 'He's gone!'

Fraser Miles walked across the yard, Jake and Nell

at his heels. 'Now, Jenny, are you sure?' he asked. 'Where's Marion?'

'She isn't here either,' said Jenny.

'Maybe she took Jess for a walk,' Matt said.

Jenny's heart began to slow down. 'Maybe she did,' she said. Then she looked around. 'But her car isn't here. She wouldn't take Jess for a walk in the car.' She looked at her father in alarm. 'What if he had another fit? What if Marion's taken him to the vet? What if Mr Palmer decides to put him down?'

Fraser Miles put a hand on her shoulder. 'Tom Palmer would never do that without talking to you about it first,' he said. 'Calm down, lass. There's probably a perfectly rational explanation.'

Matt strode into the kitchen and reappeared a moment later. 'There's a note from Marion,' he announced. 'She forgot to mention she had a hairdresser's appointment in Greybridge. Supper's in the oven.'

'Does she say anything about Jess?' Jenny asked.

Matt shook his head. 'No,' he replied. 'She doesn't mention him at all.'

Jenny looked around the farmyard as dusk crept around them and shivered. Where was Jess?

7

'Have you looked in the stable?' Matt asked.

Jenny shook her head. 'The door's closed,' she said, but she ran across and heaved open the stable door anyway. 'Jess!' she shouted but there was no answering bark, only the sound of Mercury, whinnying from his stall.

'Jenny! He's here!' her father called.

Jenny whirled round and the breath caught in her throat. Fiona McLay was coming in at the farmyard gate. Beside her was Jess.

'Jess! Oh, Jess, I thought you were lost!' Jenny cried, racing towards him.

Jess launched himself at Jenny and she hugged him tightly, rubbing her cheek against his head. Jake and Nell ran up, butting Jess, and the young sheepdog wagged his tail.

'Carrie and I took Jess with us to Puffin Island,' Fiona said, smiling. 'We had a great time. Jess loved every minute of it.'

Jenny stood up, furious. 'You took him without asking me first?' she demanded. 'How *dare* you? You've no right to do that. Jess is *my* dog, not yours!'

Fiona flushed deep red. 'But I didn't think you'd mind,' she began.

Jenny interrupted her. '*Mind?* Of course I mind!' she cried. 'Jess has been ill. How was I to know where he was? I thought he had run off and had a fit. I thought I'd never see him again. Just leave Jess alone, Fiona!'

'Wait a moment, Jenny,' Fraser Miles said, walking over to them. 'Let's hear what Fiona has to say.'

Fiona shuffled uncomfortably. 'Miss Stewart said an outing would be good for him,' she said hesitantly. 'Didn't she tell you?'

'Marion isn't here,' Matt said.

'It's no good trying to blame Marion,' Jenny put in. 'You're just trying to turn me against her, to make trouble. You've always been a troublemaker! You should never have taken Jess away in the first place – and neither should Carrie.' And, breathless, she turned on her heel. 'Come, Jess!' she called.

Jess trotted at her heels into the house. Once inside, Jenny realised she was shaking. She'd really let rip at Fiona. She bent down and gave Jess another cuddle, then looked up as she heard her father and Matt come in.

'Fiona's gone,' Fraser Miles said. 'She was pretty upset.'

'Well, so was I!' Jenny said mutinously. 'Ever since Fiona had Jess to help her over her illness she acts as though Jess is *her* dog.'

'Now, that isn't true, Jenny,' Fraser Miles said gently. 'It was a misunderstanding.'

Jenny flushed. Now that she had Jess back she was beginning to feel calmer. 'Maybe I did fly off the handle a bit,' she admitted. 'But she shouldn't have taken Jess without asking me.'

'She had permission from Marion,' Matt put in.

Jenny didn't say anything for a moment. 'Marion

wouldn't have let her take Jess without leaving a note or something,' she said.

'There's a car,' Matt said, going to the window. 'That's probably Marion now.'

Fraser turned as Marion's car drew into the yard. 'Let's ask her what happened, shall we?' he said.

Marion Stewart opened the kitchen door a moment later. Her short dark hair was newly cut and styled. 'Sorry I had to rush off like that,' she said. 'I completely forgot my hair appointment.' Then she saw Jenny's flushed face. 'Is anything wrong?' she asked.

'Did you tell Fiona she could take Jess to Puffin Island?' Jenny blurted out.

Marion looked taken aback at her tone. 'I said a run in the open air would do Jess good. He was so much better this morning and when Fiona arrived, he was so pleased to see her it seemed a pity to stop him going with her. After all, the poor thing hasn't had much fun recently.'

Fraser looked at Jenny. 'You see,' he said. 'The explanation is perfectly simple. Marion was only thinking of Jess.'

Jenny put her hand on Jess's neck and the Border collie moved closer to her.

'Why, what's wrong?' Marion asked. 'Has Jess had another fit?'

Jenny shook her head. 'He wasn't here when I got back,' she said. 'I was worried about him.'

Marion looked sympathetic. 'Oh, I'm sorry, Jenny,' she said. 'I should have thought.'

'It isn't your fault,' Jenny said. She looked at her father and Matt. 'Sorry I shouted.'

'You were upset,' Fraser said. 'But I think you owe Fiona an apology, don't you?'

Jenny nodded and put her arms round Jess again. 'Just as long as Jess is safe, that's all I care about,' she said.

Jess kept close to Jenny's side all evening, sitting under the table at her feet while they ate. Jenny and Marion had just finished the washing up when the phone rang. Fraser answered it. 'Ellen!' he exclaimed. Jenny watched her father's face as he talked with Mrs Grace. As he listened, his expression grew serious. 'Are you sure that's what you want to do?' he asked.

There were a few moments of silence as he listened, then he said, 'I think you'd better tell her yourself, Ellen.' He signalled to Jenny to come to the phone.

Jenny walked across and took the receiver from her father. 'Mrs Grace?' she said. 'Is anything wrong? Is Ian all right?'

'Hello, lass,' Mrs Grace's familiar voice greeted her. 'Everything is fine and Ian sends you his love. How's Jess?'

Jenny told Mrs Grace about the most recent fit. 'But he seems all right again now,' she finished. 'I don't understand it, Mrs Grace. I'm so worried about him.'

'You must be, lass,' Mrs Grace replied sympathetically. 'And now I'm afraid I've got something difficult to tell you. I've made up my mind to stay in Canada.'

'What?' said Jenny. 'But you can't. You belong here!'

There was a pause before Mrs Grace spoke again. 'It hasn't been an easy decision, Jenny,' she went on. 'I've thought about it a lot. But I don't think you'll be needing me back, not now you have Marion. She and your father seem to get on very well and I'm happy for them.' Mrs Grace sighed. 'My sister has been wanting me to come and live near them for a while now,' she went on. 'Perhaps that would be the best thing. My family is out here in Canada.'

Jenny swallowed hard. Did Mrs Grace think her father and Marion were going to get married? She could hardly ask with her father and Marion in the room. 'Oh, Mrs Grace, I will miss you,' she said.

Ellen Grace's voice was soft. 'And I'll miss you, lass,' she replied. 'But two women in a house is one too many. I'll ring again soon. Take care.'

Jenny said goodbye and handed the telephone back to her father. When he had said goodbye to Mrs Grace, she turned to him. 'Can't you persuade her to come back?' she pleaded.

Fraser Miles smiled and shook his head. 'I'm sorry, lass,' he replied. 'But Ellen is a grown woman. She's entitled to do as she likes. I've asked her to think it over but she must do what she feels will make her happy.'

Jenny sat down beside Jess and stroked his head. The Border collie licked her hand and thumped his tail on the floor.

'It'll be strange not having Mrs Grace at Windy Hill,' Matt said with a sigh. Then he rose. 'I'd better go and check Mercury is all right for the night.' He looked at Jenny as he went out. 'Canada isn't that far away,' he said kindly. 'Maybe you could go and visit Ellen and Ian some day, Jen.'

'That's a good idea,' Marion put in. 'I'm sure you'd love to spend a summer in Canada, Jenny.'

Jenny shook her head. 'I wouldn't be able to take Jess,' she said. 'I'd hate a summer without him.'

Marion looked thoughtful. 'I wouldn't dismiss the idea of a trip to Canada, Jenny,' she said. 'As Jess's future is a little uncertain, you might be glad to get away for a while.'

Jenny looked at Marion miserably. She didn't have to say it – what she meant was that Jess might not be around this summer.

'I thought you had some furniture catalogues you wanted to show me, Marion,' Fraser said quickly, to change the subject.

Marion smiled. 'They're in the car,' she told him. 'Can you come and help me get them? There's a whole pile.'

Jenny watched as the two of them went out of the room together. She looked down at Jess. 'Do you think Dad will marry Marion?' she asked him.

Jess licked her ear and Jenny smiled. Everything seemed to be changing around her. She was still afraid Jess might have another attack but his eyes were bright and clear. Maybe his day at Puffin Island really had done him good.

Her father and Marion approached the kitchen door, talking in low voices. But the kitchen window was open and Jenny could hear their conversation quite clearly.

'I know how much you had come to rely on Ellen, Fraser,' Marion was saying. 'But haven't you wondered what made her decide to stay in Canada?'

'What do you mean?' Fraser replied, sounding surprised. 'Her family's there.'

Marion laughed softly. 'I think it might be more than that,' she said. 'Didn't you think Ellen seemed a little uncomfortable about Anna McLay's ring going missing? Perhaps she thought Anna suspected her of stealing it.'

'That's ridiculous,' Fraser replied. 'Ellen would never do a thing like that.'

Marion spoke slowly. 'I don't know. I suppose it would be very tempting. And it isn't fair to put temptation in people's way. Have you checked Sheena's jewellery recently?'

'It never occurred to me,' Fraser said, his voice shocked. 'You can't seriously believe that Ellen is a thief!'

The voices faded slightly as Marion and Fraser entered the porch. Jenny caught her breath and sprang up as her father and Marion came through the kitchen door. 'Of course Mrs Grace isn't a thief,' she exclaimed.

Fraser Miles looked at her, his face stern. 'Have you been eavesdropping, Jenny?'

Jenny flushed but she stood her ground. 'I couldn't help overhearing you,' she said. Then she turned to Marion Stewart. 'You don't know Mrs Grace or you wouldn't say such a thing,' she protested.

Marion raised her eyebrows. 'I certainly wouldn't like to believe it of Ellen,' she said. 'But the fare to Canada *is* quite expensive . . .'

Jenny took a deep breath. 'You can't just accuse her like that. Mum's jewellery has never been locked up all the time Mrs Grace has been working here and nothing has ever gone missing. Mrs Grace wouldn't touch it. We all trust her absolutely.'

Marion shrugged.

Jenny looked at her for a moment. 'We can check if you like,' she said. 'We can do that now.' She rushed out of the kitchen and into the hall, running up the stairs two at a time, flinging open the door of her room. Switching on the light, she moved swiftly to her wardrobe and took out her mother's jewellery

box. She laid out the contents on top of the desk. Light glanced off the shiny stones and she began to go through the things. Jenny's heart began to beat faster as she lifted out the last piece of jewellery.

Her father and Marion had followed Jenny upstairs and stood in the doorway, watching.

'The aquamarine necklace isn't here!' Jenny cried. She turned to her father. 'You don't believe Mrs Grace took it, do you, Dad?'

Fraser looked at Jenny then turned to Marion and shook his head. 'You can't accuse someone without proof,' he replied.

'But you must admit, it looks suspicious,' Marion put in. 'Anna's ring has disappeared and so has Sheena's necklace – and Ellen is in Canada, intending to stay there. It would certainly make *me* think . . .'

'What's going on?' said Matt, coming up the stairs. 'I heard you from the yard, Jenny. And just listen to Jess.'

Jenny suddenly realised that Jess was barking. She ran out of the room and hung over the banister. Jess was at the bottom of the stairs, tail erect, barking loudly.

'Hush, Jess!' Jenny commanded. 'It's all right.'

Jess lay down at the foot of the stairs and gazed up at her, keeping watch, sensing that she was upset.

Jenny turned back to her father. 'You don't believe that Mrs Grace is a thief, do you?' she asked.

Matt looked shocked and his father quickly explained the situation. 'Not Ellen,' Matt concluded. 'I can't believe it of her.'

Fraser Miles looked uncomfortable. 'She's been such a help to us in the past,' he said. 'I think of her as one of the family.'

Marion just smiled. 'Perhaps you're too trusting, Fraser,' she said, laying a hand on his arm.

Fraser ran a hand through his hair. 'Now I don't know what to think,' he said.

'What are you going to do, Dad?' Jenny asked. 'Are you going to ask Mrs Grace if she stole Mum's necklace?'

Fraser shook his head. 'I couldn't do that,' he said. 'But perhaps it's for the best that she's decided to stay in Canada . . .'

Marion slipped an arm through his. 'That's more than generous, Fraser,' she said.

Jenny watched as they both turned away and went downstairs. Jess sprang up and sidled round them, coming to lie down at the foot of the stairs again.

Matt turned to Jenny and shook his head in amazement.

Jenny sighed heavily and began to walk downstairs. Jess leaped up at her and she hugged him, looking back at Matt. 'I'll never believe Mrs Grace is a thief – no matter how bad it looks for her.'

8

Over the next week Jenny had more to worry her.
Jess had another fit on Thursday afternoon and on
Friday morning, Jenny decided to stay at home. Jess
had just woken up and was still a little drowsy.

'I'll help with the lambing,' Marion offered.

Jenny looked at Marion gratefully. 'And I'll wash
up the breakfast things while you're out. It's just
that I can't bear to think of Jess getting ill again
while I'm away from him,' she said.

'That's all right, Jen,' Matt put in. 'We'll manage. You look after Jess. See you later.'

'Why don't you give Carrie a ring and ask her over?' Fraser suggested. 'You've been so busy helping me you haven't seen her for ages, have you?'

'That's a good idea,' Jenny agreed.

When the others had gone, Jenny filled Jess's bowl with water and set it down beside him. He raised his head and lapped at the dish and Jenny heaved a sigh of relief, then rang Carrie.

'I'll be right over,' Carrie promised.

Jenny settled down on the floor beside Jess. The Border collie was resting again but he had managed to drink all of his water. 'Maybe you could try eating something in a little while, Jess,' Jenny whispered to him.

When Carrie arrived, Jess opened his eyes and licked her hand.

'He's had a drink,' Jenny told Carrie. 'I thought I'd see if he wanted something to eat.'

'Good idea,' Carrie said.

'And I said I'd do the washing-up for Marion,' Jenny continued, as she picked up Jess's food bowl.

'I'll get started on that,' Carrie offered, reaching for the washing-up liquid. 'Oh, my mum uses this for her headaches,' she said, noticing Marion's packet of herbal remedy on the shelf.

Jenny nodded. 'So does Marion.' She looked at the packet. 'She'll have to get some more soon. That packet was nearly full last time I saw it.'

'But Marion hasn't been here that long,' Carrie said, looking puzzled. 'My mum's powder lasts for months and months. She only uses a tiny pinch at a time.'

Jenny put some food in Jess's bowl and went to place it back on the floor. She froze as she looked at the place where the bowl had been. There again, was the powdery mark. 'I've noticed that before,' Jenny said slowly, pointing it out to Carrie.

Still holding the packet, Carrie came to stand beside her. Jess stared at the packet in Carrie's hand and growled.

'Jess, what is it?' Jenny said, bending down to him.

Jess continued to stare at the packet. Carrie reached down and touched a finger to the powder on the floor then held it against the clear plastic of the packet. 'It looks like the same stuff,' she said slowly. Carrie tipped a little of the powder from the packet into her hand. 'It *is* the same,' she concluded.

Suspicion began to dawn in Jenny's mind. 'That powder has been sprinkled over Jess's food,' she said.

'It certainly looks that way,' Carrie replied quietly.

'Oh, Jess!' Jenny cried. 'Is this what's been making you ill? You were right, Carrie. It *was* something he ate.' She turned to the other girl. 'But why would Marion do a thing like this?' Jenny asked, unwilling to believe Marion could be so cruel. 'Maybe Jess ate some accidentally.'

'But accidents like that don't happen more than once, do they?' Carrie replied. 'Look, Jenny, I think we should take this stuff to show to Mum. She'll be able to tell us more about it.'

Jenny nodded. 'The sooner the better,' she agreed. 'Let's go!'

'I know the powder is dangerous unless taken in exactly the right quantity,' Mrs Turner said when the girls showed her the packet. 'I can't imagine Marion having used so much of it for headaches. Mine lasts for ages. Maybe she spilt it,' Mrs Turner went on. 'You would have to ask a herbalist exactly what effect it would have if taken in large doses. I get my supply from the herbalist in Greybridge.'

Jenny nodded. 'We'll do that. Thanks, Mrs Turner. We'll go right now.'

'I'll phone Fiona,' Carrie said. 'She can meet us at the bus stop.'

'Fiona?' Jenny echoed.

'You don't mind, do you?' Carrie asked. 'We'd planned to meet this afternoon anyway, and as it's about Jess, she'll want to come along. She's been phoning me to ask how he is because she didn't like to phone you.'

Jenny looked at Jess, standing by her side. Fiona really did love him and Jenny regretted the things she had said to Fiona the last time she had seen her. 'OK,' she said. 'Fiona too.'

An hour later Carrie pushed open the door of the herbalist's shop in Greybridge.

'I'll stay outside with Jess,' Fiona offered.

Jenny nodded and gave Jess a quick pat before following Carrie into the shop. Jars and bottles lined the shelves and there was a huge glass flask on the counter filled with dark liquid. The shop smelled of herbs and spices. A woman in a white coat smiled at them from behind the counter. 'How can I help you?' she asked.

Jenny took the packet out of her pocket and handed it over nervously. 'We wondered if you could tell us about this,' she said.

The woman took the packet and tipped some of the contents on to the palm of her hand, then looked at them curiously. 'Where did you get this?' she asked. 'I wouldn't sell this to children.'

Jenny opened her mouth to answer but Carrie interrupted. 'We found it,' she said quickly. 'The label had your shop's name on it and we were worried in case it might be dangerous so we brought it in to see what it was.'

Jenny looked at Carrie in surprise but the herbalist was smiling. 'You did the right thing,' she approved. 'Taken in the right quantities this substance has remarkable healing properties. A very small amount can be effective for pain relief. But if the dosage is wrong it can have very dangerous side effects.'

'What kind of side effects?' Jenny asked, her heart beating a little faster.

The woman shrugged. 'That varies,' she said. 'Very often it causes extreme drowsiness – but that's only if the dosage is wrong. And it can cause sickness and fever – even fits. It was very sensible of you to bring this in. I'll just hold on to it. We wouldn't want anyone taking it accidentally.'

Jenny swallowed. 'I suppose if an animal found it and took some it would be really dangerous,' she said.

The herbalist nodded seriously. 'A dog or a cat could suffer a great deal if they took this by accident. It could eventually kill them.'

Jenny swallowed again and Carrie touched her arm. 'Come on, Jenny,' she said.

The herbalist smiled. 'Thank you,' she said. 'You did the right thing bringing this in.' She frowned slightly as she looked at Jenny. 'Are you all right? You look a little pale.'

Jenny managed to nod and smile until she was outside. She put her arms round Jess and he licked her face. 'Oh, Jess, you might have died,' she said.

Carrie told Fiona what had happened in the shop. 'It's really hard to think Marion would poison Jess deliberately,' she continued as they walked down the street.

'Let's go for a walk down by the river and think this out,' Jenny suggested.

They turned on to the river walk and Jenny let Jess off the lead. He scampered ahead of them, snuffling at the bushes and barking at the ducks on the water.

'He looks all right now,' Fiona said. 'Maybe he *did* get hold of the stuff by accident.'

'Every time he had a fit?' Jenny asked. 'No, it can't be that. He always had the fits when Marion was looking after him. She must have put that stuff in his food. Why else would there be some on the floor round his dish?'

'Why would Marion want to poison Jess?' Carrie asked. 'I thought she liked Jess.'

'But Jess doesn't like *her*,' Jenny replied.

Fiona looked worried. 'I don't think Marion is as nice as she pretends, Jenny,' she said. She flushed. 'I know you thought I was trying to turn you against her that day we took Jess to Puffin Island but it was Marion who told me to take him. I just dropped in to see if you had changed your mind about coming. Marion said you were too busy helping with the lambing and you wouldn't mind us taking Jess. . . . And there's something else I haven't told you.'

Carrie picked up a stick and threw it for Jess. The Border collie raced after it.

'What?' asked Jenny.

'When I arrived I knocked on the kitchen door but nobody answered,' Fiona went on. 'The door was open slightly so I just assumed you were upstairs.'

'Go on,' Jenny said.

'Of course, you weren't there,' Fiona said. 'But Marion was.' Fiona stopped.

'You'll have to tell us the rest now, Fiona,' Carrie urged.

Fiona flushed slightly. 'I went upstairs, thinking that you might be in your room, Jenny.'

'Then what happened?' Jenny asked.

'Marion was coming out of your bedroom,' Fiona told her. 'She was stuffing something into her pocket, but she was so surprised to see me she dropped it on the floor.'

'What was it?' Jenny asked, shocked.

'A necklace,' Fiona replied.

Jenny gasped. 'A necklace! One of Mum's necklaces is missing. Marion said Mrs Grace must have taken it. Can you remember what the necklace was like?'

'It was a gold chain with pale blue stones set in it,' Fiona replied.

'But that's it. That's the one that's missing!' Jenny cried.

'So *Marion* stole it!' Carrie put in. 'But why on earth would she want to steal one of your mum's necklaces?'

'Perhaps she wanted to get Mrs Grace into trouble,' Fiona suggested. 'The way she got me into trouble with Jenny for taking Jess away.'

'It looks to me like Marion was trying to turn you against Mrs Grace as well, Jenny,' Carrie said.

Jenny thought for a moment. 'You've always said that Marion wanted to marry Dad,' she said to Carrie. 'And Mrs Grace thinks they will get married. I think that's why she's decided to stay in Canada.'

'And Miss Stewart wanted Jess out of the way too,' Fiona put in, 'because she doesn't like him, and Jess can sense that.'

'And she knows that I wouldn't be friends with her if I thought Jess had a problem with her. So by poisoning him she's been able to put Jess's hostility down to his illness!' Jenny exclaimed. 'But why didn't you tell me all this before?'

Fiona shook her head. 'I didn't think you would believe me,' she explained. 'You seemed to be getting on so well with Marion and after I brought Jess back you were so angry. And anyway, why should anyone believe me? Especially you, Jenny. After all, I set fire to Windy Hill and I've been really rotten to you in the past.'

Jess scampered up and offered his stick to Jenny. Jenny bent and rubbed his ears, taking the stick. 'I'm sorry I lost my temper like that,' she said to Fiona. 'I should have listened to you.'

'And I should have told you about Marion and the necklace sooner,' Fiona said. Her face grew distressed. 'Maybe if I had spoken out earlier Jess wouldn't have got so sick. Marion would have been forced to stop poisoning him.'

Jenny frowned. 'Well, she can't poison him any more,' she said. 'She doesn't have the herbs.' She shook her head. 'I should have taken more notice of Jess. He saw the danger in Marion.' Jenny jumped up.

'Where are you going?' Carrie asked.

'Back to Windy Hill,' Jenny replied. 'Marion isn't going to get away with this.'

'You mean you're going to accuse her?' Fiona asked. 'But you don't really have any proof – and, according to what you told me, the herbalist said that those herbs *could* be used for headaches.'

'I don't care. I'm going to tell her I know what

she's been up to,' Jenny said firmly. 'Then she won't dare to try and harm him again.'

Fraser, Matt and Marion were back by the time Jenny got home.

'Where have you been?' Matt asked, rubbing Jess's ears as the Border collie ran to him.

'Greybridge,' Jenny replied, looking at Marion.

'With Jess?' said Marion. 'He certainly seems to have recovered well.'

Jenny looked at her smiling face and reminded herself that this woman had tried to poison Jess. Looking at Marion's pleasant expression, it was hard to believe. 'If he *is* better it's no thanks to you, Marion,' she said.

Fraser Miles looked up from the newspaper he was reading. 'What did you say, Jenny?' he said as if he couldn't believe his ears.

'I said it was no thanks to Marion that Jess is better,' Jenny insisted. She turned to Marion, then took a deep breath. 'I took your headache powder to the herbalist in Greybridge. She told me what happens if it's given in the wrong quantities. And I know you've been giving it to Jess. You've been poisoning him!' At the sound of

Jenny's strained voice, Jess ran to her, pressing against her leg.

'Jenny!' Matt exclaimed, his face shocked.

Jenny lifted her chin and looked at Marion, her hand protectively on Jess's head.

Marion opened her eyes wide. 'How dare you accuse me of that? I'm shocked at you, Jenny.'

Jenny flushed. 'You were giving those herbs to Jess,' she said quietly. 'That's what made him sick.'

Marion put her hand to her head. 'Oh, Jenny, I wish you hadn't stolen my herbs,' she said. 'All your shouting has brought on another headache. Fraser, I must go and lie down.'

Fraser turned to Jenny. 'Jenny, go to your room,' he said.

'But, Dad,' Jenny protested. 'I'm telling the truth! She really has been trying to poison Jess. You've seen how Jess behaves around her.'

'Jenny!' her father thundered. 'Do as you're told! I think you've caused enough trouble for one day with your ridiculous accusations. Look what you've done to Marion.'

Jenny looked at Marion standing behind her father. She had her hand to her head but, as her eyes met Jenny's they were steely and cold. 'Don't be hard on her, Fraser,' she said. 'All you have to do is phone the herbalist. She'll tell you those herbs are a headache remedy. Jenny is so upset about Jess needing to be put down she doesn't know what she's—'

'Jess *doesn't* need to be put down!' Jenny interrupted hotly.

'Jenny!' her father warned. He turned back to Marion. 'It's very good of you to look at it that way,' Fraser said to Marion. 'Is this true, Jenny? Are the herbs a headache cure?'

'Yes, but . . .' Jenny began.

'That's enough,' her father said. 'Go to your room.'

Jenny looked helplessly from her father to Marion. He didn't believe her. And if he didn't believe her about this then he would never believe her about the necklace. Marion stared back, her eyes triumphant. She knew she had won. She knew Fraser was on her side. Jenny looked once more at her father. 'Dad?' she said desperately.

Fraser Miles regarded her coldly. 'I told you to go to your room, Jenny,' he said. 'We'll talk about your behaviour tomorrow when you've calmed down.'

Jenny turned, defeated. Fiona had been right. She had no proof and she had failed – she had failed Jess.

9

Jenny was up early next day, determined to try to talk to her father before Marion came downstairs. As she entered the kitchen Jess ran to her and she bent to pat him, not at all surprised to find him so well.

'Of course you're well, Jess,' she whispered to him. 'Marion hasn't got her herbs any more, has she?' She smiled in spite of her worries. Jess's eyes were bright and he wagged his tail furiously as she hugged him.

Matt was stacking plates from the table on to the worktop by the sink. He turned to her. 'You know, you really should try to get on with Marion,' he said. 'She's doing her best to help us.'

Fraser Miles came into the kitchen as his son finished speaking. 'I want you to apologise to Marion when you see her,' he told Jenny. 'She's spending the morning in bed. She still has a headache but she's coming out with us this afternoon to help with the lambing.'

Jess moved closer to Jenny, warned by Fraser Miles's tone that she was in trouble. Jenny reached a hand down and buried her fingers in the soft fur at his neck but she said nothing. It was obvious that her father was still very angry with her.

'Well?' he said. 'You will apologise, won't you?'

Jenny swallowed. 'But, Dad, you don't understand . . .' she began.

Fraser looked at her impatiently. 'I understand that you don't like Marion and that you're determined to push her out of Windy Hill,' he said. 'It isn't good enough, Jenny. We've got trouble with the lambing and I'm too busy to put up with any more nonsense from you.'

'What trouble?' Jenny asked, alarmed.

Fraser ran a hand through his hair. 'We have a rogue ewe,' he told her. 'I've found several lambs dead – killed.'

Jenny gasped. She knew that sometimes a ewe would kill her lamb for no apparent reason – but several!

'You mean this ewe is killing other lambs – lambs that aren't her own?'

Matt nodded. 'We're going to try and weed her out but it could take days to cover the whole flock. Don't make any more trouble, Jen.'

Jenny nodded. 'I thought I'd go over to Dunraven today,' she told her father. 'I'll take Jess with me.'

Fraser gave her a brief nod. 'That would be best,' he said. 'But when you come back I'll expect you to apologise to Marion. Think it over, Jenny. I'm serious about this.'

Jenny watched as her father and Matt left, calling to Jake and Nell. If any sheepdog could find a rogue ewe, it would be Nell, she thought. Jenny hoped she could do it. Losing lambs was a serious business.

Jenny turned from the window and put some bread in the toaster. She wished she could be out in the fields, helping – but not if Marion Stewart was going to be there.

★

Fiona came out to meet Jenny as she arrived at Dunraven. Carrie had already arrived. Jess jumped up and Fiona made a fuss of him. 'What happened when you got home yesterday?' she asked, as they made their way into the kitchen.

'Did Marion confess?' Carrie asked eagerly.

Jenny shook her head. 'Dad didn't believe me and Marion denied everything, then said that Jess really should be put down. It was terrible.'

Fiona looked at her with concern. 'But she can't have Jess put down,' she said.

'She won't,' Jenny said determinedly. 'I'm going to keep him with me all the time so she'll never get another chance to poison him. If he doesn't have any more fits, he'll be safe. But I'm scared. What happens after the Easter holidays when I'm at school?'

'Mrs Grace will be back by then,' Carrie assured her.

'No she won't,' Jenny said desolately. 'Marion has turned Dad against Mrs Grace too, remember? So he's not going to encourage her to come back from Canada.'

Anna McLay appeared at the door. 'Hello, Jenny,'

she said as Jess trotted over to meet her. 'Did I hear you saying that Ellen was staying in Canada?'

Jenny nodded. 'All her family is out there now,' she said. 'And besides . . .' she stopped.

Anna McLay looked concerned. 'What is it, Jenny?'

'Miss Stewart thinks that Mrs Grace stole your ring,' Jenny blurted out. 'She told Dad that was why she had decided not to come back.'

Anna McLay looked shocked. 'But that's ridiculous!' she said. Then she flushed. 'Oh, this is my fault. I'm so sorry. I should have remembered to tell you. I found my ring.'

'What?' said Jenny. 'When?'

'A few days ago,' Mrs McLay replied. 'I was taking a pair of trousers to the cleaners and I found it when I was clearing out the pockets. I must have slipped it in there when I was doing some housework and forgot all about it. I really should have mentioned it before.'

'That's all right,' Jenny said excitedly.

Mrs McLay left and Jenny turned to the others. 'This makes all the difference. If I tell Dad that, then he'll know that Mrs Grace isn't a thief.'

'And maybe he'll realise that Marion could be wrong about other things too,' said Carrie.

'Lying about them, you mean,' Fiona put in.

Jenny nodded and called Jess. 'Wait till Dad hears what I've got to tell him, Jess,' she said, bending to give him a cuddle.

'Would you mind if I came back to Windy Hill with you later on?' Fiona asked.

'Of course not,' Jenny replied. 'But why?'

Fiona flushed slightly. 'I still feel guilty about not mentioning seeing Miss Stewart with your mum's necklace,' she said. 'If I could tell your dad what I saw, then it might help.'

Jenny smiled. She still couldn't quite get used to the idea that Fiona would want to help her. 'That's really thoughtful of you, Fiona,' she said.

Jess reached up and laid his head in Fiona's lap.

'Jess trusts you, now,' Jenny said. 'And so do I.'

Fiona blushed even more. 'It's time I did something for you,' she said awkwardly. 'You've done such a lot for me.'

'I'll come too,' Carrie announced. 'After all, you might need some moral support.'

Jenny laughed. 'I reckon I'll need all the support I can get, Carrie.'

Carrie looked at her, for once serious. 'You only have to ask,' she said.

Jenny nodded. 'I know that,' she said. She knew now that she and Carrie would always be friends – and Fiona was proving to be a good friend too. How could they fail to persuade her father they were telling the truth?

When Jenny pushed open the kitchen door at Windy Hill late that afternoon, her heart sank a little. Her father and Matt were sitting opposite each other at the kitchen table with Marion between them – and they looked exhausted. Fraser Miles's head was down and he was staring into his coffee cup, his thoughts obviously far away. Marion looked round as the girls came in and gave them an unfriendly look. Her usually immaculate hair was windblown and untidy and she had a smear of mud across one cheek.

Matt looked up and smiled but he looked utterly weary. 'Hi, Jen. Hello, girls,' he said. 'I hope you've had a better day than we've had.'

Jenny sat down at the table and Carrie and Fiona followed her. 'Did Nell manage to find the rogue ewe?' she asked.

Fraser shook his head. 'Not yet,' he said shortly. 'We found four more dead lambs today.' He ran a hand through his hair. 'That sort of thing has never happened at Windy Hill before. I can't help but think it's a bad omen.'

Marion laid a hand on his arm. 'Sheep farming is such hard work, Fraser,' she said sympathetically. 'Have you ever thought of giving it up? Windy Hill would fetch a good price. You'd probably never have to work again. You could relax, take holidays, do something else if you wanted to.'

Jenny gasped. 'No!' she burst out. Seeing the shocked expression on Matt's face, she turned to watch her father's response. His face too seemed frozen with shock, then he moved his arm so that Marion's hand was no longer resting on it. 'Leave Windy Hill?' he said. 'Sell it? I don't think you understand what the farm means to us, Marion.'

Marion flushed slightly but she recovered quickly and stretched over to lay her hand on his arm again. 'Oh, I know you love farming,' she said. 'But surely there are less demanding jobs? You're so talented, you could do anything.'

Fraser gave an incredulous laugh. 'That's very complimentary of you, Marion,' he said. 'But you don't understand. Sheep farming is my life. I could never give it up. And besides, Windy Hill isn't mine to sell.'

This time, Marion drew back her hand. 'What do you mean?' she said, her voice sharp. 'I thought you owned it.'

'I do own it during my lifetime,' Fraser said. 'But Windy Hill belonged to my wife's family. It's held in trust, to be handed down to Matt.'

Jenny smiled at Carrie and Fiona in relief.

'You!' Marion exclaimed, turning to look at Matt.

Matt frowned. 'Why should that upset you, Marion?' he asked. 'If you're interested, I can assure you that I would never sell Windy Hill either. There will always be Mileses at Windy Hill. It's our home.'

Marion tried to smile, but couldn't quite manage it. 'Oh well,' she said, 'it's been a hard day and I feel one of my headaches coming on.' She rose and turned away. 'In fact, I think I had better go home. I have a feeling my headaches are going to prevent me coming to Windy Hill – for the foreseeable future. I'm not sure all this hard work is for me.'

Fraser looked concerned, then his eyes hardened as he realised what Marion was really saying. 'I think I understand, Marion,' he said. 'Don't let us keep you.'

Marion nodded. 'I'll go and pack,' she said, making for the door.

Jenny looked at her father. He looked even more weary than he had earlier. 'I thought she was interested in me and my family – not in how much the farm might be worth if she could get me to sell it,' he said, shaking his head sadly.

Jenny was concerned at the disappointment she could see in her father's eyes. Had he really liked Marion so much?

A few minutes later, Marion appeared again, carrying her two suitcases.

'I'll see you out,' Fraser said quietly. 'Thank you for everything you've done.' He took the cases from Marion and followed her out to her car.

Suddenly Jess darted after them. Jenny leaped up. 'Jess!' she called.

Carrie and Fiona followed Jenny to the door and Matt came up behind them.

Marion was at the boot of her car, changing out of her wellingtons into shoes. Jess bounded over to the boot, hackles up, growling.

'Jess! Here, boy!' Jenny called again.

Jess ignored her. He was pulling at a rolled-up scarf that was hanging over the edge of the boot.

'Jess!' Fraser Miles called sharply.

Jess turned at once, the scarf caught in his teeth. It unravelled slowly and, as Jenny watched, something glinted as it fell to the ground. 'It's Mum's necklace!' she exclaimed, running over and picking it up. She held it out to show her father.

Fraser Miles's eyes were flinty as he looked at Marion. 'What are you doing with this necklace?' he demanded.

'I don't know how it got there,' Marion protested. 'I've never seen that scarf in my life.'

'So what was it doing in the boot of your car?' Fraser asked frostily.

Marion flushed. 'I don't know,' she stammered. 'Unless Ellen Grace put it there. I wouldn't put it past her. After all, that woman's a thief.'

Jenny clutched her mother's necklace in her hand and turned to face Marion Stewart. 'Mrs Grace isn't a thief – *you* are!' she cried. 'Mrs McLay *found* her ring. Nobody stole it. Mrs McLay just mislaid it. But you stole Mum's necklace and tried to put the blame on Mrs Grace!'

Marion looked down her nose at Jenny. 'Don't make accusations you can't prove,' she snapped.

'But she *can* prove them,' Fiona said, stepping forward. 'At least, I can! I saw you coming out of Jenny's bedroom with that necklace the day you told me to take Jess to Puffin Island. You were stuffing it into your pocket.'

'This is outrageous!' Marion blustered. 'How dare you call me a thief?'

'You aren't only a thief,' Carrie declared, taking a step towards Marion Stewart. 'You tried to poison Jess.'

'You wanted us all to think that Jess was dangerous,' Jenny said, her voice strained. 'You wanted him put down. You wanted him dead — either poisoned or destroyed.'

Marion snatched her scarf from Jess, wrenching it out of his mouth. Her hand caught against his teeth and the dressing she had worn on her wrist for so long flapped loose. Jenny's eyes widened as she saw the clear, unblemished skin beneath the dressing. 'Jess didn't bite you at all, did he?' she breathed. 'You put that bandage on your wrist just to make us think he was dangerous.'

Fraser looked at Marion in disgust. 'You weren't interested in me or my family at all, were you, Marion?' he said. 'You didn't care about the things we think are important. You just wanted me to marry you, then sell Windy Hill to provide you with an easy life.' He shook his head. 'To think I nearly fell for it. You had me convinced that Ellen was a thief. You even tried to turn me against my own daughter.' He cast a quick look at Jenny and she put her hand in his. He grasped it tightly then turned once more to Marion Stewart. 'It's time for you to leave,' he said shortly. 'And please don't come back!'

Marion slammed the boot shut and strode round to the front of her car. Without a backward glance, she got into the driver's seat, started the engine and roared off.

Fraser squeezed his daughter's hand. 'I should have listened to you, lass,' he said wearily.

Jenny bent and called Jess to her. The Border collie came running and she hugged him fiercely. She could hardly bear to think how close she had come to losing Jess.

10

As Marion Stewart's car disappeared into the distance, Fraser Miles turned to Jenny and Matt. 'Come on,' he said. 'We've got something to do.'

'What's that?' asked Jenny.

'I'm going to phone Ellen to ask her to come back to us,' Fraser replied.

Jenny smiled up at him. 'Do you think she will?'

'I hope so, lass,' her father said, striding towards the house. 'I certainly hope so.'

Carrie grinned. 'Fingers crossed,' she said.

'Mum has been missing her a lot, too,' Fiona agreed, as they all followed Fraser inside.

Everyone crowded round the telephone as Fraser rang Canada. 'Ellen?' he said when someone answered. 'I've rung to ask you to come back. We need you.'

Jenny heard a surprised exclamation on the other end of the line and listened carefully as her father explained about Marion Stewart, then he handed the phone to her. 'Ellen wants to speak to you,' he said.

Jenny took the phone and smiled as Mrs Grace's voice came over the line. 'Oh, Jenny, what a terrible time you've been having,' the housekeeper said. 'I must say, I never liked that Marion Stewart, but I thought your father was very taken with her. In fact I expected to hear they were getting married and there would be no room for me at Windy Hill any more. So I thought the best thing to do was to make a life for myself out here in Canada.'

'But you'll come back now, won't you?' Jenny asked anxiously.

'Your father certainly seems to want me back,'

Mrs Grace replied. 'He says he misses my cooking,' she laughed.

Jenny looked up at her father. 'It isn't just your cooking,' she said. 'We miss *you*. We all miss you.'

There was a short silence before Mrs Grace spoke again. 'You don't know how glad I am to hear that,' she said at last.

'And you'll come home?' Jenny asked again.

'Home,' Mrs Grace repeated. 'That sounds nice. Yes, Jenny, I'll come home.'

Jenny passed the phone back to her father and turned to the others, beaming. 'She's coming home!' she said.

Matt grinned. 'Thank goodness for that!' he said. 'I don't know about anybody else, but I'm starving!'

Jenny laughed and Carrie made for the fridge. 'Come on, Fiona, let's cook a celebratory tea for us all,' she said.

Matt rolled his eyes. 'What have I done?' he asked. 'Thank goodness Vicky is coming tomorrow. At least she can cook!'

'She can help with the lambing too,' Jenny said happily. 'And Mrs Grace will be home soon.'

'I can't wait,' said Matt.

★

'She's picked something up,' Matt said three days later as Jenny stood beside Vicky, watching Nell. The sheepdog moved forward, body close to the ground, creeping in among the flock. Jenny had Jess on his lead by her side. The Border collie's ears were pricked, all his attention on Nell.

'Do you think she's found the rogue ewe?' Vicky breathed.

Fraser Miles stood watching his dog, his eyes intent. Jake was waiting patiently by his side while Nell searched, combing the flock, separating one sheep from the rest, then rejecting it. But this time the dog seemed to be on to something.

'I think she might have,' Fraser said, moving forward. 'Stay here, you three. Keep Jess with you, Jenny.'

Jenny put her hand on Jess's neck and watched, fascinated, as her father walked towards Nell with Jake at his heels. Nell was among the flock now, moving quietly so as not to disturb the ewes and their lambs.

Then Jenny saw Nell crouch down and fix her eyes on one particular ewe. It stood there for a moment as if mesmerised, then it slowly began to move towards the dog. Nell rose swiftly and nudged the ewe out of the flock, herding it towards Fraser Miles. Fraser murmured to Jake and the sheepdog moved behind the ewe, ready to turn it if it bolted. Fraser reached out and caught it by the scruff of the neck, then he turned briefly. 'Bring the rope, Matt,' he said.

Matt walked slowly forward, a rope in his hand. He slipped it round the sheep's neck and secured it.

Fraser Miles bent and rubbed Nell's ears. 'That'll do, Nell,' he said softly. 'Good dog!'

Jenny raised her hand from Jess's neck as Jake and Nell trotted over. Jess nuzzled the bigger dogs, wagging his tail.

'Isn't Nell wonderful?' Jenny said to Vicky.

Vicky smiled. 'Jake and Nell are both wonderful sheepdogs in their own way,' she said.

Fraser Miles nodded. 'You're right, Vicky,' he agreed. 'But Nell is a bit special. Jake is a good outrunner, the best I've ever had, but Nell can pick a bad one out of a whole flock. Not many dogs can do that.'

'Jess is like Nell,' Jenny said thoughtfully. 'He picked out Marion Stewart, didn't you, boy? He knew she didn't belong at Windy Hill.' Jess butted

Jenny's hand and licked it, looking up at her adoringly.

'So he did, Jenny,' Fraser Miles replied, smiling. 'Jess is a grand dog too.'

Matt led the ewe over to the jeep at the edge of the field and loaded it on to the trailer.

'What will happen to it, Dad?' Jenny asked.

'It will have to be destroyed,' Fraser Miles told her. 'Once a ewe starts trampling lambs there's nothing else for it.'

The afternoon was growing dark and the wind was rising off the sea. Jenny looked around the fields. They were dotted with ewes and tiny Blackface lambs. 'It's been a good lambing hasn't it, Dad?' she asked.

Fraser smiled. 'Even better than last year,' he said, his eyes moving over his flock.

Jenny lifted her head and let the wind blow through her hair. Then she looked down at Windy Hill, lying snug and safe in the valley below.

'Come on,' said her father. 'Let's go home.'

They were halfway down the track to the farm when Jess sat up, ears pricked, and began to bark.

'What is it, boy?' Jenny asked, as Matt slowed down for a corner.

Jess continued to bark, scrabbling at the door of the jeep.

'He wants out,' Vicky said. 'You'd better stop, Matt.'

Matt stopped the jeep and Jess leaped out. 'Wait for me!' Jenny called, jumping out after him.

Jess ran round her feet, then raced away from her, turning to make sure she was following.

'Go on, Jenny. We'll follow,' her father said, as Matt started the engine again.

Jenny raced the last few metres towards the farm gate and hurtled through it. Jess was already at the kitchen door, still barking. Jenny stumbled in surprise. Light was flooding out of the door, spilling into the yard and, as she ran again towards the house, a figure appeared in the doorway. Jess leaped up at the figure, his tail wagging furiously.

'Mrs Grace!' Jenny yelled, throwing herself across the doorstep. 'Oh, it really *is* you. You're back!'

Ellen Grace caught Jenny in her arms, hugging her as Jess tried to climb up the housekeeper's legs. Mrs Grace bent down, gathering Jess to her. 'I managed to get an earlier flight,' she said breathlessly as Jess licked her face.

Jenny looked at the familiar face. Mrs Grace's hair

was tousled and her cheeks were flushed. 'We didn't expect you yet,' she said, hugging her again as she stood up.

There was the sound of a vehicle pulling up and Jenny turned to see her father, Matt and Vicky getting out of the jeep.

'Ellen!' said Fraser, his face breaking into a smile as he came towards the housekeeper.

Mrs Grace went to meet them. Matt threw his arms round her then looked up, his eyes going to the kitchen door. He sniffed. 'I smell something cooking,' he said.

Vicky laughed. 'What a welcome, Ellen,' she said.

Ellen Grace laughed back. 'It's the best welcome I could have,' she replied.

Jenny laughed and bent to hug Jess. 'Jess likes having you home too, don't you, Jess?' she said. Jess barked and licked Jenny's ear.

'We *all* do,' said Fraser Miles, shepherding everyone into the kitchen. 'Welcome home, Ellen.'

Jenny closed the door on the darkening afternoon and turned towards the cosy warmth of the kitchen. 'Now we really are *all* back at Windy Hill,' she said. Then, turning to her Border collie, added, 'And it's all thanks to you, Jess!'

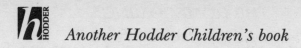

PIGS AT THE PICNIC
Animal Ark Summer Special

Lucy Daniels

Mandy Hope loves animals more than anything else. She knows quite a lot about them too: both her parents are vets and Mandy helps out in their surgery, Animal Ark.

Mandy and James have won a working holiday at a rare breeds farm. They have a great time helping out with the animals and getting the farm ready to host an important fundraising picnic. Then all the arrangements start to go wrong – especially when the farm pigs get involved! It seems that someone is trying to sabotage the event. But who?

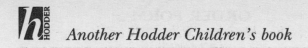

TABBY IN THE TUB
Animal Ark 41

Lucy Daniels

Mandy Hope loves animals more than anything else. She knows quite a lot about them too: both her parents are vets and Mandy helps out in their surgery, Animal Ark.

A feral tabby cat has turned up in Welford and Mandy is worried. The poor thing is about to have kittens and she has no one to look after her. Bill Ward, the postman, comes to the rescue, allowing the tabby to make herself at home in his garden shed. And, before long, the tabby is able to return the favour in a very special way . . .

ORDER FORM

Lucy Daniels

0 340 70438 1	JESS THE BORDER COLLIE 1: *THE ARRIVAL*	£3.99 ❑
0 340 70439 x	JESS THE BORDER COLLIE 2: *THE CHALLENGE*	£3.99 ❑
0 340 70440 3	JESS THE BORDER COLLIE 3: *THE RUNAWAY*	£3.99 ❑
0 340 73595 3	JESS THE BORDER COLLIE 4: *THE BETRAYAL*	£3.99 ❑
0 340 73596 1	JESS THE BORDER COLLIE 5: *THE SACRIFICE*	£3.99 ❑
0 340 73597 x	JESS THE BORDER COLLIE 6: *THE HOMECOMING*	£3.99 ❑

All Hodder Children's books are available at your local bookshop, or can be ordered direct from the publisher. Just tick the titles you would like and complete the details below. Prices and availability are subject to change without prior notice.

Please enclose a cheque or postal order made payable to *Bookpoint Ltd*, and send to: Hodder Children's Books, 39 Milton Park, Abingdon, OXON OX14 4TD, UK.
Email Address: orders@bookpoint.co.uk

If you would prefer to pay by credit card, our call centre team would be delighted to take your order by telephone. Our direct line *01235 400414* (lines open 9.00 am–6.00 pm Monday to Saturday, 24 hour message answering service). Alternatively you can send a fax on *01235 400454*.

TITLE		FIRST NAME		SURNAME	

ADDRESS	

DAYTIME TEL:		POST CODE	

If you would prefer to pay by credit card, please complete:
Please debit my Visa/Access/Diner's Card/American Express (delete as applicable) card no:

Signature .... Expiry Date: ....

If you would NOT like to receive further information on our products please tick the box. ❑